# HIRED FOR ONE TUSCAN SUMMER

JESSICA GILMORE

Recycling programs for this product may not exist in your area.

ISBN-13: 978-1-335-47088-1

Hired for One Tuscan Summer



For questions and comments about the quality of this book, please contact us at CustomerService@Harlequin.com.

Harlequin Enterprises ULC
22 Adelaide St. West, 41st Floor
Toronto, Ontario M5H 4E3, Canada
www.Harlequin.com

HarperCollins Publishers
Macken House, 39/40 Mayor Street Uppe
Dublin 1, D01 C9W8, Ireland
www.HarperCollins.com

**Printed in U.S.A.**

1 2 3 4 5 6 7 8 9 10 HDC 28 27 26 25

**Passport to Paradise**

*Final destination: happily-ever-after!*

The heat is rising, adventure is calling... So why not strap in and get swept away to the world's most luxurious locations? Lands of white sands, blue skies—and sizzling nights...

Follow our intrepid travellers as they check their baggage and lose themselves in first-class romance. But are their connections just for the summer... or are these jet-setters en route to their five-star forever afters?

Grab your ticket for...

*Marriage Ruse in Paradise* by Susan Meier

*Hired for One Tuscan Summer* by Jessica Gilmore

Available now!

And keep your eye on the departures board for...

*Faking It for the Cameras* by Justine Lewis

*Surprise Reunion in Croatia* by Ella Hayes

*One Bed Between Rivals* by Joss Wood

and more, coming soon!

Dear Reader,

What if the best night of your life turns out to be the worst? That was the starting point for this Italian reunion romance set in gorgeous Tuscany and the idyllic Amalfi coast. Liv has never quite got over her one night with her artist crush, or the way he left her without a word, so the last thing she wants is to bump into him again at her brother's wedding, especially when it transpires that he owns the gorgeous wedding venue. As for Luciano, life took an unexpected turn for him that night, a turn which meant putting his own needs and wants firmly behind him—until Liv shows up in his office and brings the past crashing back. Add in a demanding bride, Liv's high-achieving family and a wedding in need of a bilingual planner, and the ingredients are there for a sun-soaked summer fling.

I loved getting to know Liv and Luciano and spending time in his gorgeous Tuscan castello and island near Positano. I hope you do too.

Love,
*Jessica*

Incorrigible lover of a happy-ever-after, **Jessica Gilmore** is lucky enough to work for one of London's best-known theatres. Married with one daughter, one fluffy dog and two dog-loathing cats, she can usually be found with her nose in a book. Jessica writes emotional romance with a hint of humor, a splash of sunshine, delicious food—and equally delicious heroes!

**Books by Jessica Gilmore**

**Harlequin Romance**

***Billion-Dollar Matches***

*Indonesian Date with the Single Dad*

***Fairytale Brides***

*Reawakened by His Christmas Kiss*
*Bound by the Prince's Baby*

***The Princess Sister Swap***

*Cinderella and the Vicomte*
*The Princess and the Single Dad*

***A Five-Star Family Reunion***

*Christmas with His Ballerina*

***Blame It on the Mistletoe***

*Miss Right All Along*

***Summer Escapes***

*Fake Date on the Orient Express*

*Christmas with His Cinderella*
*It Started with a Vegas Wedding*

Visit the Author Profile page
at Harlequin.com for more titles.

For Sheila

Thank you for everything.

# CHAPTER ONE

*R*IGHT. *H*ERE WE GO.

Olivia Davenport, Liv to everyone apart from her family, old headmistress and newly ex-boss, stepped out of the taxi, a neutral smile readied on her lips. A smile she intended to keep in place over the next week. Her lack of ambition: *Darling, surely you should have made partner by now, it's important to make an impact early in corporate law, you know?* Neutral smile. Her single status: *You'll be thirty soon, darling. It's time to be a little less romantic, hmmm?* Ditto. Watching her sister-in-law-to-be ramp up to infinity on the bridezilla scale? Ditto, ditto, ditto.

She would even remain neutral and calm when she put on the fuchsia silk, mermaid-style bridesmaid dress which clashed horribly with her hair and complexion and made her feel like an over-stuffed sausage bursting out of its skin.

*Smile, Olivia Felicity Davenport, smile.*

The late-afternoon sun was almost unbearably bright; Liv adjusted her sunglasses as she took in her surroundings. The Castello Del Visconti. Del Visconti, that was a name she hadn't heard in a long time—a name she had done her best to forget she had ever heard in the first place. But the Del Visconti she knew had been an artist, not the owner of an actual real life castle and— *No*, she scolded herself. She was *not* going to spend another minute thinking about him or the one perfect night they had shared. A perfect night that had turned into a perfect nightmare.

Pushing her memories back into the locked vault where they belonged, Liv turned her attention back to the Castello, trying to ignore the exaggerated grunts from the taxi driver as he theatrically heaved her suitcase out of the boot with a scowl. Maybe she should tell him that only half of the contents were hers, the rest—and heaviest—essential items that Annabel, the steely-eyed bride-to-be, had instructed Liv to bring with her.

*Honestly*. Liv already had one overbearing older sister and one overbearing sister-in-law. It wasn't fair of Max to saddle her with another. But as she took in the terraced gardens on both sides of the driveway, the thick, turreted medieval stone tower in front of her and the acres of vineyards and olive trees all around, the whole framed by rolling Tuscan hills, the bluest of skies and permeated by the scent of pine, jasmine and citrus, Liv felt her spirits start to lift. Yes, she was about to spend an entire week with her extended family, yes, she was at the mercy of a sister-in-law who believed that the *maid* in *bridesmaid* was to be taken literally, especially when said bridesmaid was merely a sister-in-law-to-be without a title or drop of blue blood in her ancestry, and yes, she was still wrestling with the not-that-unexpected bombshell her boss had dropped on her last week, but this really *was* glorious countryside. It had been far too long since Liv had last visited Tuscany. It was time to make new memories in this beautiful place.

'Olivia, there you are.'

*Neutral smile*, she chanted silently as Liv turned to greet her brother and his bride, visions in matching neutral, perfectly ironed linen, Annabel's hair sleek and bouncy despite the heat. Liv could feel her ponytail sticking to her neck already.

'Here I am,' she said brightly. 'What a gorgeous venue! You really couldn't have picked anywhere more perfect, the views on the way here were stunning.' She accepted the double air kiss with which Annabel invariably greeted her before giving her brother a warm hug. She might have some reservations about his taste in wives, but Max had always been her favourite family member—even if the bar was pretty low. 'And this Castello, wow. It is incredible.'

Annabel's perfectly made-up mouth thinned. 'It looked larger in the photos.'

'Right.' Liv managed not to raise her eyebrows as she looked again at the sweeping driveway lined by cypress trees, the flower-filled terraces which cascaded down the hillside in front of them and the Castello itself, a square tower guarded by four turrets which formed the centre of the main house, flanked by two sizeable wings which had clearly been added on at a later date. *Small* wasn't the first adjective that came into her mind. Nor the hundred and first. 'Never mind, I'm sure we'll squeeze in somehow.'

'*And*,' Annabel continued. 'I was assured that I would have a dedicated wedding planner on-site for the full week but when I got here no one seemed to know where this Elisabetta is. I am having to deal with the *housekeeper* instead.'

'Elisabetta is the owner's sister,' Max explained. 'But apparently, she's been called away. The timing is less than ideal, poor Annabel is stressed enough as it is.'

'Right,' Liv repeated, the only word that seemed safe right now. Of course, Annabel would want the daughter of the house catering to her whims rather than someone who was *paid* to do so.

'But luckily Francesca seems very competent, our suite is lovely—' Max continued, oblivious to his fiancée's chilly expression.

'Francesca's English is frankly not of the standard I would expect from someone dealing with international clients, she lives off site and I am struggling to get her to reply to the simplest of questions.' Annabel cut her groom off ruthlessly. 'Thank goodness you are here, Olivia. I wish you had flown out yesterday like I suggested, but better late than never.'

'Thank goodness *I* am here?' Neutral was forgotten, replaced by incredulity. Annabel had made it clear that Liv belonged at the bottom of the bridesmaid pecking order, fit for bringing heavy items but not much else.

'You speak Italian, don't you?'

'I can get by but…'

'And you have managed events?'

'I was social secretary of my university Italian club once upon a time if that's what you mean, but that was years ago…'

'I'm sure it's like riding a bike. You speak the language, you understand event planning…'

'One university ball!'

'You'll be the perfect person to act as liaison with the venue over the next few days. Now come to my room. I have a list of questions I need you to get answers to.'

Liv looked pointedly at her bag, a hint Annabel ignored but Max, bless him, recognised.

'Darling, I think we should let Olivia settle in first, she's been travelling all day.'

Annabel gave Liv the kind of sweeping glance that made her all too aware of every damp strand of hair, her shiny forehead and nose and crumpled, travel-stained top.

'You have half an hour,' she said finally before turning on her heel and stalking off, pulling her phone out of her pocket as she did so.

Max gazed after her, his forehead creased with worry. 'She'll be making more voice notes. Don't mind, Annabel, she just wants everything to be perfect and the non-appearance of this Elisabetta has thrown her. You will help her, Liv, won't you? For me?'

Liv suppressed a sigh. She had decided to arrive a day earlier than the rest of her family, *not* because she was happy to be a courier and general dogsbody but because she had intended to spend some time exploring the countryside and picturesque Tuscan villages and towns, to return to Florence for the first time in nearly a decade and indulge in a nostalgia fest in the city she had spent such a memorable year in. She could have taken time *after* the wedding, but getting one week off from her demanding job had been difficult; two had seemed impossible. Maybe that wouldn't have felt like such a burden if she had actually *enjoyed* her job, but the truth was she had only done her law conversion course and taken the job in the respected City law firm because it had felt like the right thing to do. Expected of her by her high-achieving family, who thrived under pressure and found their jobs in-law fascinating. Liv had only ever wanted to fit in, but once she had started work she had felt more alone than ever.

Not that that would be a problem anymore. A mix of anticipation and fear stole over her. She'd felt caged in by the demands of her job and had dreamed of freedom. Now that she was free she needed to decide what to do next. There were so many possibilities, each more enticing than the last, none involving negotiation and clauses. Travel, further study, a totally new career in something she had never thought about before. All of the above?

Deciding was a problem for next week. This week's problem was ensuring none of her family found out about her summary firing—*negotiated pay-off* in the firm's language. A not inconsequential sum of money in return for packing up her desk, handing in her pass and departing the building without a fuss. She did not want her news to overshadow her brother's wedding. Besides, she needed a way to spin it to minimise the drama as much as possible.

'I'll help where I can,' she said at last, unable to resist the plea in her brother's eyes. 'But I have no intention of being at Annabel's beck and call all week. That's *your* job, you're the one marrying her not me.'

'Thanks, sis, you're the best.' Max picked up her case and let out an *oof.* 'Why have you bought rocks to my wedding?'

'That will be the ten pairs of shoes your lovely bride dropped at my flat last week and insisted I bring.' Liv picked up her overnight bag and garment carrier. 'Right, where to? The dungeon? The servants' quarters? A rustic shepherd's hut outside the castle walls?'

'Originally you were between Mum and Dad and Portia and Celeste. I said *originally*,' he repeated as Liv let out a groan. 'I moved you to one of the courtyard rooms. I thought you would appreciate the privacy.'

'Max, you would be my favourite brother even if you weren't my only brother. Thank you.' A week sandwiched in between her parents and her perfect older sister and her perfect older sister's even more perfect wife was too hideous to contemplate.

She followed Max as he took a hedged path through the garden and around one of the wings of the house. Four stories high, long and narrow with shuttered windows, the wings were an elegant addition to the solid medieval keep. 'This wing is the one they let for weddings and events, along with the converted accommodation in the courtyard at the back,' her brother explained. 'The main part of the house and the other wing are for the family.'

'Good of them to spare twenty bedrooms or so. What do they do?'

'Own land as far as the eye can see and have

done for generations, make wine and olive oil, host weddings, just your usual castle-owning activity.'

'Nice work if you can get it.'

The path led them to a huge courtyard flanked by orchards, beyond which were more gardens. The courtyard buildings had obviously once been workshops and stables but since converted into accommodation.

'The pool and gym are that way, the walled garden where the wedding will be is through there and that door takes you into our wing. We have all the facilities we need there including a sitting room, a dining room and a kitchen filled with snacks and drinks you can help yourself to,' her brother explained. 'Just make yourself at home basically.'

'Max, this really is incredible.' Liv stopped to readjust her bag, tilting her head to take in the beautiful building and inhale the citrus-sweet smell emanating from the orchards.

'Annabel's parents wanted her to have her perfect wedding so here we are. We're pretty lucky.'

'I'll say.' Liv couldn't compute how much hiring a place like this for a week would cost. And Max's in-laws' generosity didn't stop with the wedding. There was a sizeable deposit on a house in Surrey as a wedding gift too. Not to be outdone, her parents had paid for the honeymoon, two weeks in the Maldives, as well as a cheque with several noughts at the end to help with furnishing the five-bedroom three-bath home. Her parents had always been generous. As long as their offspring conformed to their idea of how to be a functioning adult, that was. Only as far as she could tell neither Portia nor Max had ever considered or wanted to do anything other than following in the family law tradition. It was only Liv who had struggled, who had dreamed of escape, who had done something different for a while, studying art history including a year here in Italy, even if she had done what was expected in the end, tired of always feeling like she was on the outside, emotionally battered and bruised from her time in Florence, needing to feel like she belonged. But maybe it was time to embrace that outsider status, not run from it.

'Okay, this is you.' Max handed her a key and pointed to an open stone archway, beyond which Liv could see a wooden staircase winding upward. 'Let me see if I can get a crane to winch this suitcase through the window…'

'Ha very ha!' But Liv was relieved it was

Max, not her, hauling the case up the stairs. Her brother waited, panting slightly, for her to open the door and deposited the case just inside. His phone pinged as he did so and he fished it out of his pocket and looked at the screen.

'Annabel is summoning me. Will you be okay if I head off and leave you to settle in?'

'Go, go, I'll be fine,' Liv reassured him. 'I'll unpack, sniff out the kitchen you mentioned and grab a drink, explore, see if I can find the pool. Don't worry about me.'

'Perfect, that all sounds lovely. The thing is…' Max shifted uncomfortably. 'Annabel is really counting on you to help her out. She has quite a long list of questions for the staff and Francesca has been a little elusive today. The sooner she gets some answers the easier it will be for her to relax.'

Liv mentally translated *quite a long* to *exhaustive* and stifled a sigh. 'I'm sure I can sort everything easily and then we can *all* relax. Give me an hour and I'll come find you. Promise.'

Ushering her apologetic brother out of the door, Liv turned to take stock of her home for the next week, and despite her work problems and the prospect of a week playing translator and problem solver for Annabel her spirits lifted. 'Nice,' she breathed aloud. 'Very nice.'

The room was simple, painted white on three sides, the fourth the natural golden stone the whole courtyard was built in with two wide, deep windows cut in, both cushioned, allowing the room's occupant to sit and watch the comings and goings in the courtyard below. On the other side doors opened onto a small iron balcony furnished with a small round table and chair, with views over the garden and the hills beyond. Liv flung them open and breathed in the late-afternoon air, looking out over the beautifully designed landscape with pleasure. To one side she caught sight of what must be the pool; on the other a flash of white alerted her to the wedding venue, a pergola apparently situated in flower-filled gardens.

Leaning on the balcony rail, Liv inhaled again, slow and deep, allowing the sweet-scented air to calm her before stepping back into her room. It was simply but tastefully furnished. A large bed dominated one wall; on the opposite side sat a comfortable-looking easy chair with a low table in front of it, perfect for a morning coffee—or a bedtime aperitif. Bright rugs softened the polished floorboards.

She opened a door and found it led into a small dressing area, which in turn led into a comfortable bathroom furnished with soft towels and an array of expensive toiletries. A basket next to the full-length mirror in the dressing area held a state-of-the-art hairdryer and a complicated straightening and curling tool. Everything had been thought of and provided.

What Liv *wanted* to do was sink into the easy chair and take a few moments to relax. She eyed it wistfully but turned away resolutely. If she sat down now, she would never force herself back up. Instead she quickly unpacked, hanging the still-fuchsia bridesmaid dress on a hook in the dressing area and disposing of her own belongings into the various drawers, transferring Annabel's into a separate bag, which she left by the door for her sister-in-law—or more likely Max—to recover. Five minutes with the anti-frizz spray trying to repair her hair and a dash of mascara, powder and lip gloss later Liv was ready.

'Olivia Davenport reporting for duty,' she said, regarding herself critically in the mirror and trying not to sigh faced with her decidedly unswishy hair. She would have to do.

Liv headed down the stairs, across the courtyard and into the main house through the door Max had indicated earlier. To one side she could see the dining room, a tempting-looking coffee pot and platter of grapes and cheese set up on the sideboard, to the other a large sitting room with several cosy clusters of chairs and sofas. At least they *would* be cosy if it wasn't for the three straight-backed people sitting on the chairs nearest the door, looking as if they were waiting for an unpleasant appointment.

Liv cast one longing look at the cheese and coffee and turned instead into the sitting room, the neutral smile she had perfected ready on her lips.

'Major and Mrs Anstruther-Jones. How lovely to see you.'

Annabel's father got to his feet to shake her outstretched hand, but Annabel's mother merely nodded at Liv. She had made it clear from the outset that Max was lucky to be marrying Annabel, especially as her daughter was the granddaughter of a baron. Every time Liv was with Annabel's family she couldn't help thinking of the Elliots in *Persuasion*, puffed up with pride and formality.

Was it too late to kidnap her brother and hide him away until he came to his senses?

'Finally,' Annabel said. 'Didn't Max tell you I needed you straight away?'

*Yes, I have settled in, thank you, my room is lovely. No, I am happy to help, don't mention it.* Liv managed not to say the words but just thinking them made her feel better.

'I am just going to get some coffee,' she said instead. If not *actually* happy she *was* reconciled to helping but she was damned if she would let Annabel walk all over her.

Liv didn't deliberately linger but nor did she hurry, filling a small plate with a few olives, some grapes and a few slivers of cheese and pouring herself a generous mug of coffee. She took the refreshments through to the sitting room and chose a seat at right angles to the Anstruther-Joneses, as she didn't want to feel like she was being interviewed, and inhaled the scent of the ambrosial coffee. Then, and only then, did she look at the increasingly impatient Annabel.

'Okay,' she said. 'What exactly is the problem and what are you hoping I can do about it?'

Luciano Del Visconti stared around his sister's office. If glaring made things magically spring into place then the room would be in perfect order, but instead the roomy office remained a mess, the filing haphazard at best, and as for the booking system? Utterly incomprehensible. He should have known better than to trust his younger sister when she had informed him that she had the wedding side of things completely in hand and he could leave everything to her.

No, he could berate himself later. The most important thing was to figure out exactly what was and was not happening with the wedding taking place this week and then the tall, unpleasant Englishwoman might stop haranguing his staff.

Although, there was *another* wedding booked in for next week and another the week after that and so on and so on right until the autumn. A never-ending stream of perfectionist brides, angry grooms and pushy parents. What had he been thinking? The Castello Del Visconti had existed for hundreds of years without any need to host weddings; why change things now?

Only… Elisabetta had needed a project of her own when she decided against going to university and she had been so enthusiastic about the Castello's potential. She had spent her last year at school researching the local competition, even getting a weekend job at a nearby venue before working up a fully costed project proposal. She'd thrown all her time and energy into turning the Castello into a wedding venue and for the last couple of years had succeeded so admirably Luciano had pretty much left her to it. His mistake.

As was not seeing the signs that she wasn't coping.

He crossed over to the open window and stared out unseeing, his mind running rapidly through the options. He wasn't going to be able to run the weddings himself, not with the rest of the vineyards, estates and holdings to manage, not to mention the other, more low-key events the Castello had always hosted. Wedding planning wasn't Francesca's job and although she was doing her best, the language barrier this week wasn't helping, and from what he could make out from Elisabetta's notes all the forthcoming few bridal parties were English or American, which meant that barrier wasn't going to be broken anytime soon. Besides, Francesca was a miracle worker but he couldn't expect her to do two full-time jobs. No, the only answer was to find a temp. A bilingual temp with good organisational skills and, he thought as he turned and looked around the untidy room, someone who enjoyed problem solving. How hard could it be?

Because even if Elisabetta reappeared as suddenly as she had disappeared she still clearly needed back up. Maybe a permanent assistant. He sighed again. His little sister might be twenty-one but he was still worrying about her. It was hard to let go.

His gaze fell on a photo on the cluttered desk: he and Elisabetta were posing next to the old wine press, holding a magnum of wine, the first of the new variety he had introduced. Her smile was wide, her hair whipped by the wind. Looking at it no one would know how much she had struggled since the accident.

A knock on the door recalled him to his surroundings and most immediate problems. 'Come in,' he said and braced himself for Francesca and her long list of woes. A substantial bonus and the promise of extra holiday when all this was over was keeping her onside for now, but she looked more rebellious every day. If she walked out as well, then he was *completely* screwed.

'Ah, excuse me, Signor Del Visconti?'

Luciano looked up from the photo. The Italian was fluent but the accent unmistakably

English. Instead of the dark-haired Francesca, the woman who entered the room was pale with long, straight, reddish hair, her nose dotted with freckles—and she was very familiar. His pulse sped up as he stared at her in shock.

Grey eyes widened at the sight of him and she took a step back. *'Luciano?'* The disbelief was clear in every syllable, in the shock in her eyes, on her expressive face.

Luciano was immediately transported back to another time, another place, another him. A time of paint and canvases, late lazy lunches, evenings filled with wine and talk and laughter. A carefree time. And one night. A night when he and she… His whole body tightened at the memory.

'*Liv?* What are *you* doing here?'

'My brother, Max, is getting married and Annabel asked me…' She stopped, half shook her head. 'Sorry, I'm not making sense. I'm actually looking for…' She stopped again, paled. 'You. I think I am looking for you.'

# CHAPTER TWO

SAY SOMETHING, *ANYTHING*. But try as Liv might, intelligible words wouldn't come. The last time she had seen Luciano Del Visconti she had been eight years younger, coming to the end of her year abroad studying at the University in Florence as part of her art history degree.

Not that her age and reason for being in Florence were the salient part of the memory which left her paralysed, unable to speak coherently, to move or think. Last time she had seen Luciano she had also been naked and he…he had been gathering up his clothes, clearly desperate to leave her bed and her as quickly as he had tumbled into it.

Nine months of hopelessly crushing on the tall, dark and handsome artist upstairs, several hours of complete happiness when it looked like she was embarking on her very own Italian love story, only for the whole thing to turn into the type of humiliating memory she kept very firmly locked away.

At least she *had* kept it locked away. It was hard to do so when all six-foot-something of humiliation was standing right in front of her.

Even worse he looked better than ever, whereas she really needed a shower, had the start of a headache and hair so flat it could double as a runway.

'*Del Visconti*,' she said finally. 'Why didn't I guess?'

'Liv,' he said again, and her stomach clenched. Luciano might have changed, matured, become even more handsome if such a thing was possible, the last of the boyishness replaced by a not unattractive hardness. But his voice. Oh, his voice was just the same, low with a hint of gravel, the accent twisting itself around her name, making it sound like a caress. *No*, she was not going to think about caresses. Nor was she going to ask him why he had left her so abruptly eight years ago, left his flat, left Florence and never contacted her again. She swallowed back the questions that had haunted her for nearly a decade and tilted her chin, channelling Annabel as best she could.

'I am here to try and sort some things out.

It seems that my brother and his fiancée are not getting the level of service they were expecting. Their contact, Elisabetta, is apparently missing, is that right?'

His eyes hardened. 'My sister is not *missing*, she is just not here. However Francesca is very competent and I can assure you that the quality of service will not be affected.'

'Apparently her English isn't that fluent and Annabel doesn't speak Italian.' She would *not* sound apologetic.

'But you do…'

Damn that voice and damn the way it warmed her whole body. 'Yes. So if you can point me in the direction of Francesca I can try and get some answers to Annabel's twenty questions and leave you in peace.'

'Francesca will no longer be dealing with this wedding.'

'Oh? Does that mean Elisabetta is returning?' She crossed her fingers. Annabel could take back control, and she could leave this room and put Luciano back into the locked box of past mistakes where he belonged.

'No, it means that I will be looking after the wedding and as you know my English is more than adequate.'

'*You* are?' Her imaginary box sprung open

again, memories and feelings tumbling out. This was the *last* thing she needed or wanted. It was bad enough to know that Luciano was in the same building as she was, even a building as large as the Castello, but if he took over the wedding there would be no escaping him—or the memories. 'But you're an artist. What do you know about weddings?'

For a moment his expression flickered, a wave of such sorrow clouding his eyes she took an involuntary step forward to comfort him, but then he blinked, and the cool, professional mask was back.

'Oh, but I am no longer an artist. I am CEO of Del Visconti holdings, the Castello, the vineyards, the wine, the property, all of it. So, you see, a small affair like a wedding will be no problem at all.'

Liv hesitated. She owed Luciano nothing good. If *anything* she owed him revenge. And what better revenge than to stand aside and watch him try to manage Annabel and her parents' expectations. It would be delicious.

And she would have a ring side seat.

But this was Max's wedding too and she loved her brother even if she deplored his taste in fiancées and in-laws. And, if she was being honest, his dress sense.

'My sister-in-law,' she said carefully, 'is demanding.'

'So am I.'

'She wants every aspect of this wedding to be perfect.'

'As will I.'

'She will expect someone at her beck and call, 24/7. It sounds like you have a lot on your plate. Can you really give her the time she needs?'

'Your sister-in-law has been in my Castello for two days and in that time, she has made Francesca cry three times that I know of. If it was up to me, I would demand you all leave right now and I would cancel the rest of the summer's weddings, but my sister has worked hard to build up this business.'

'The sister who isn't here?'

'And my lawyer told me the contract is non-negotiable and my publicist threatened to resign if I gave her an upset bride to deal with, so reluctantly I will continue with the booking. But I will not allow my staff to be spoken to in that way, which is why I shall now be the main liaison.'

'You won't have to. I will be the intermediary.' As soon as the words were out Liv wanted to recall them. Only…maybe she hadn't reacted rashly after all.

'You? Why?'

'Because my brother wants this wedding to go well and for Annabel to be happy and I can make that happen.' And because that way *she* could deal with Francesca and ensure she steered well clear of Luciano in the process.

And because if she was busy, she would have an excuse to duck out of the myriad dinners and other organised fun.

And if she was busy, she would have a ready-made excuse to avoid her parents and sister, which meant the chances of them finding out about her temporary unemployment status had suddenly lengthened.

It actually made sense.

But clearly not to Luciano, whose eyes narrowed. '*You?*' he repeated. Liv didn't know why the disbelief in his voice stung. It was hardly the first time he had made it clear she was, well, nothing. But she was a very different woman to the twenty-one-year-old infatuated student she had been back then. She tilted her chin.

'I am a qualified lawyer dealing with complex negotiations every day.' Okay, an unemployed lawyer but he didn't need to know that.

'I am sure liaising with one wedding planner on one wedding won't be too onerous.'

Luciano's mouth tilted into something that might be a smile. 'I meant, don't you want to enjoy the wedding rather than spending a week helping organise it? The countryside is beautiful around here.'

'I know. I lived not far from here for nearly a year, remember?' Their eyes met, a connection, a joint memory of that time, and Liv could feel her cheeks start to heat. 'Listen, you have met Annabel and her family. The rest of the guests won't be too dissimilar...' Including her own family. 'I had hoped to be able to explore on my own, but I think I realised even when planning some day trips how unlikely it was I could escape easily. Annabel will have me at her beck and call whether I like it or not. So, let's use that and make everyone's life a little easier.'

Luciano didn't reply but his gaze was thoughtful and Liv fought the urge to squirm under it. It was as if he saw through her. But she knew that look and the promise of intimacy of old and would not be fooled again. Instead, she tilted her chin and gave him the much-practised neutral smile. 'Or not. I am happy to leave you to manage Annabel alone if you really insist.'

'Come on,' he said at last. 'Let me introduce you to Francesca and then we can discuss if this will work.'

Liv obediently followed Luciano as he led her down the corridor. It was amazing how much this part of the Castello looked like a normal office, the room he took her to filled with several rows of desks, each equipped with a monitor and keyboard. There was a functional kitchenette at one end holding several mugs and the ubiquitous office microwave and kettle. All completely familiar until she looked out of the arched leaded windows at the gardens and vineyards beyond, until she looked back into the high-ceilinged corridor to see narrow windows peering defensively across the valley beyond. The Castello was in a perfect position; no invading army would be able to approach unseen.

'The first two floors of this wing are offices,' Luciano explained briefly as he walked at speed along the corridor. 'I run the whole business from here, the estate, the vineyard, the family holdings.' Whatever *they* were but Liv was already too awed to speak. It was hard to reconcile this sharp-suited, well-groomed, confident owner of all he surveyed with the scruffy, paint-covered artist she had known. Luciano still had the same intensity about him, but that was the only similarity with his younger self she could see.

'Family apartments are in the old Castello, guests and staff on the top two floors here. As you see we have given the courtyard and the other wing over to weddings and other hires.'

*And what about art, what about your studio, where is that?* she wanted to ask. Liv could still see the vivid splashes of colour, the way Luciano had conjured up the vibrancy of the Tuscan countryside with a slash here and a line there, unformed, unstructured and yet clear. His talent had blazed off the canvas.

But it was too intimate a question. It came too close to acknowledging what had been between them no matter how briefly. Far better to stick to facts as she rapid-fired questions trying to figure out the set-up. How many guests could the Castello accommodate, did they cater on-site, how many permanent staff, how many temporary workers, how about health and safety, licences? Her detail-orientated brain kicked in, creating the distance she so desperately needed whilst memories knocked at her consciousness demanding a reliving. Later maybe. When she was safely alone. Then maybe she could replay that year.

Replay the hellos in the courtyard, the first, tentative conversation in her then-halting Italian, the spontaneous glass of wine one late autumn evening, the morning-coffee routine they fell into, the gradual ripening of friendship, the charged moment that changed everything. The moment it all fell apart. But not yet. Not here. Not with Luciano beside her, keeping a respectful distance, but still close enough to touch.

Her hands clenched into fists.

*Don't think about touching.* Don't remember just how sure his touch had been, the feel of him under her fingertips. How, despite the way it ended, that night had been her north star, the one no other had lived up to.

Don't remember how everything had felt so very right when it clearly had been so very wrong.

The worst part was that she had thought they were friends. But friends didn't treat each other like that. Didn't leave each other humiliated and alone, questioning their judgement, their memories, every interaction and word, scouring for clues as to what had happened. It had taken her a long time to trust her judgement again, to let anyone in, always on the look-out for the moment it would all fall apart.

Worst of all, no man, no matter how kind or thoughtful or attractive, had made her heart beat as fast as Luciano had, had set her pulse and body alight in the same way.

'I see,' she said, her voice too loud, too bright, glad he couldn't read her mind. 'This is all very impressive and you are very clearly busy. I'll make sure I don't bother you again once you have introduced me to Francesca. It's been nice to see you again…' *Liar.* 'Thank you for everything.'

Luciano turned to face her, his expression incredulous. 'Liv, you are staying in my home, have offered to liaise with my staff. This will not be the last time we see each other.'

'Maybe not.' *Unfortunately.* 'But this is Max and Annabel's occasion, I don't want anything to detract from that, so it's best if we forget that we ever knew each other before. To avoid awkward questions.'

Questions like *How exactly* do *you know the heir to the Del Visconti empire?* and *Why have you never mentioned him before?* and *How did you lose touch?*

'Forget we knew each other?' Luciano repeated, his voice flat.

'Exactly. Strangers. It shouldn't be hard. After all, you…' She bit off the words before she could say them. Expose herself.

'After all I what?'

*Forgot about me. Ghosted me. Left me.*

'Nothing. It doesn't matter. Look, I know my family, they can be intense and I just want to fly under the radar this week. So, let's not complicate things.'

He continued to stare at her, inscrutable, and Liv tilted her chin, maintaining eye contact, trying to appear completely unaffected by his proximity, by this unexpected reunion. 'Fine,' he said eventually. 'If that is what you want. Francesca is just along here. I'll introduce you and then leave.'

'Good, glad we are on the same page.' Liv was proud of her tone, light, airy, as if she didn't care what Luciano thought, but despite her best intentions her mind was working furiously. He sounded surprised, as if she was the one being unreasonable. When *he* was the one who just upped and left.

Well, if Luciano Del Visconti thought she was the same naive girl who had crushed on him one Florentine year he was in for a rude awakening. Liv might make plenty of mistakes, but she never made the same mistake twice. Especially where her heart was concerned.

Luciano still couldn't quite believe that Liv Davenport was here in his home, in his offices, but it was soon clear that Liv's offer to act as a liaison between Luciano's beleaguered housekeeper and the bridal party was a welcome one, and by the time Luciano left them to it, Francesca and Liv had established a good rapport and his presence and input were both unnecessary. Thank goodness. Liv perched on the end of Francesca's desk to tackle Annabel's long list of complaints. Luciano listened just long enough to realise that Liv had been right when she had been incredulous at his plan to take the wedding planning over. He just didn't understand why perfectly respectably sized candles were too short or why one shade of pink ribbon was preferable to another identical-looking shade. This was Elisabetta's territory, not his.

The thought of his sister resurrected the never quite dormant sense of guilt and worry, and as he headed back to his office he pulled his phone from his pocket to see if she had responded to his last message. No, nothing since yesterday's terse fine. Once again, he cursed himself for not seeing the signs earlier, not intervening before they had got to this stage. She and Salvio hadn't seemed that serious but the break-up had been hard on her. Even if Luciano had been secretly relieved, he had never felt that their playboy neighbour was good enough for his little sister. Added to which she had doubled her workload with weddings, one after another taking up the whole summer. And of course, she always struggled around the anniversary. How could it be eight years since she had been pulled, barely alive, out of the crash which had killed her parents, Luciano's own father and beloved stepmother? Eight years since the coma and the long, painful rehabilitation, the follow-up surgeries, the nightmares. No one looking at the confident, beautiful twenty-one-year-old would guess that she still regularly woke up screaming for her mother.

But Luciano knew. It was his job, his duty to take care of his little sister and he had failed.

So, he wouldn't bombard her with messages, or try to guilt her into replying. She needed time and space and there was nothing he would deny her.

Which meant employing a temp for the

rest of the summer and a fervent thank-you to whatever deity was in charge of weddings that this particular wedding had brought Liv to his door, list in hand and ready to help.

Liv, colder, more formal than he remembered but still as beautiful, that beat of attraction as steady as it had been all those years ago despite her distance. Liv, who he hadn't seen since…since the night of the accident.

Luciano swore under his breath.

*Of course*. The accident had been so all-encompassing, the aftermath so devastating, the impact on his life so absolute that the world before sometimes seemed like a dream. His studio apartment, the days spent painting were a fantasy life half remembered. The people he had known strangers.

But Liv hadn't been a stranger. Far from it. He'd been attracted to the slight redheaded English girl the first time he had seen her, reading in the courtyard of their shared building, utterly absorbed in her book. An attraction that had only grown as he had got to know her. An attraction that had led inexorably to that night, to a drink, to a first kiss, to the kind of sex he hadn't experienced before or after. And he had left her without a word. Good God, it was a miracle she hadn't thrown a glass of water over him and walked away to watch him suffer the whims of her sister-in-law. It was the least he deserved. She might yet, because one thing was clear. He owed her a long-overdue apology. Another thing to add to the to-do list.

Luciano returned to his own office, smaller than his sister's, infinitely tidier, but he found it difficult to settle down to the myriad tasks awaiting him. Instead, his eyes kept being drawn to the view, at once so familiar and yet always so breathtaking. A view that always reminded him of his responsibilities, of the many livelihoods that depended on his success, his commitment. It wasn't often that Luciano thought about all he had given up, allowed himself to think about the smell of paint, the feel of a paintbrush in his hand, the way time would disappear when he put paint to paper. After all, what was the point? Remembering changed nothing. All he could do was exactly what he had been doing since he had received that fateful phone call. One foot after another, one day after another, focusing on what was, not what might have been.

And that was exactly what he should be doing now. But despite all his best intentions Luciano found it impossible to concentrate and closed his laptop with an impatient snap, heading outside to the orchard, stopping only to collect a beer on the way. The offices had emptied out while he had wasted precious time procrastinating, the only staff left on the premises those who lived in or who were looking after the wedding party. Another item to add to his to-do list: he should, he knew, invite the happy couple and their families to dinner the next night, play the expansive host, organise a wine tasting, and he would. But not yet. For now, he simply wanted to be alone.

Sunset was late at this time of year, the light golden, bathing the tree-covered hills, imbuing the orchard with the magical quality of a midsummer's evening. The air was fragrant, the intense heat of the day softening to a gentle warmth, and as Luciano inhaled, he felt some of his disquiet slip away. He couldn't change the past and wouldn't change the decisions he had made. This might not be the life he would have chosen but it was the life he had, and it was one many would envy, He had a thriving business, wealth, a family name which commanded respect all over the world. He still had his sister despite coming so close to losing her too. There was a lot to be grateful for. So this occasional sharp sense of loss, of displacement, was nothing but an echo of a former life, one he had almost, almost forgotten. One stirred up by the unexpected arrival of someone from that past life. That was all this momentary disquiet was.

Luciano walked slowly through the trees until he reached a small clearing on a hill, a beautifully carved bench situated in the perfect spot to take advantage of the views. Beside it two cherry trees provided welcome shade. He and Elisabetta had commissioned the bench and planted the trees on the first anniversary of the crash. He knew his sister came here often. They both felt closer to their parents here than in the formal graveyard with the imposing family mausoleum.

He leaned against the bench and took a sip from the bottle, savouring the solitude until the sound of footsteps warned him that he was no longer alone. He turned, scanning the direction he had heard the sound emanate from until, with a feeling of inevitability, a familiar figure appeared in the small glade.

Liv. Of *course* it was Liv. They had always had a knack for choosing the same place at the same time. Some things had clearly not changed.

She didn't see him at first, since he was

half hidden by the tree. She'd changed into a striped sundress, her hair washed and falling down her back, and for a moment he was transported back to the courtyard in Florence and the ever-growing awareness of the long-legged English girl in the studio downstairs. She was no longer a girl but a woman, maturity adding soft curves to the slim frame.

For a moment he thought about trying to slip away, giving her the privacy she probably needed after a day travelling before being catapulted into the role of wedding planning and a shock and probably unwanted reunion. But then she turned and her whole body stiffened. She had seen him and it was too late to retreat.

'Liv.' He pushed off the tree. 'Everything sorted with Francesca and your sister-in-law?'

'Luciano.' Her gaze fell onto the bench and its simple inscription and her cheeks reddened. 'I'm sorry, this is clearly a private place. I'll leave you in peace.'

'No, stay.' The words came out as a command and he added, 'Please. You are very welcome here.'

'I… Okay.' she slowly walked towards him; he sat down on one side of the bench, and after a guarded glance she joined him.

'I only have the one…' He held up the still-cold beer. 'But I am happy to share.'

Liv looked startled and then laughed. It was the first time he had seen her smile since she had arrived and once again it was as if he had stepped back in time.

'Do I look that desperate?'

'Not at all, but you have had quite the day.'

'I have, that's true. Luckily Francesca is lovely, just clearly overwhelmed, which is understandable. I think between us we can manage.'

"Thank you for stepping in, especially on your vacation.'

'Luciano.' She widened her eyes in mock solemnity. 'This is not a holiday, it's a wedding. Besides, I don't mind. Like I say, it keeps me out of the way of my family and the way things are going soon I'll have too much time on my hands.' She eyed the beer and then held out her hand. 'Actually, I will have a swig if you don't mind.'

Luciano handed her the bottle and she wiped the top before taking first a sip and then a longer drink, with a grin. 'Oh, that is good. I was going to get myself a drink but Annabel and her parents were in the dining room and I wasn't up to an interrogation. I should head back and face them, I suppose, especially if I am going to get any dinner.'

He studied her for a moment, the shadows below her eyes, the resignation in her expression. 'Or you could eat with me,' he said abruptly. 'Would that be the lesser of two evils?'

'The lesser of *what*?'

'Isn't that the right expression?' Luciano had been brought up bilingual thanks to his New Zealander stepmother and the needs of the winery, which exported across the English-speaking world, but for a moment he doubted himself until she laughed again.

'It is. I've just never heard anyone use it about themselves before.'

'Liv.' He couldn't put it off any longer. 'I am aware I am probably the last person you wanted to see and I am *very* aware that I more than owe you an apology.'

She didn't look at him, her gaze fastened on the bottle she still held, her cheeks a deep pink.

'It's okay.'

'No, it's not. I am very sorry about how I left things, how I left you in Florence. I would like to explain if you would let me.'

'There's no...' She stopped. Straightened. 'Actually yes, I would appreciate that, as you said I am staying here in your home, liaising with your staff. Maybe clearing the air is the right thing to do.'

It was always an effort looking back to before, like stepping through a portal to another world, another Luciano. 'This bench,' he said a little abruptly. 'These trees. They are here as a memorial, as a place for Elisabetta and I to remember.'

'It's a beautiful spot.'

'That night. I needed water.'

Liv stilled. He obviously didn't need to clarify which night.

No need to recount how he had woken up with Liv in his arms and the conflicting emotions that had assailed him. Tenderness, lust, joy that they dance they had been engaged in had finally led them to this place. But also apprehension. Because Luciano wasn't a man who entered into anything lightly. He wasn't sure if he wanted a relationship at all, nor did he want to ruin their friendship, and after all Liv would be leaving Italy in just a few weeks.

But primarily joy. Because it had felt so right.

'No.' He tried to gather his thoughts. 'It starts before. It starts with Meg.'

*'Meg?'* She frowned, confused.

'Elisabetta's mother.' He smiled. 'Meg was the most incredible person. She had been brought up on a farm in New Zealand which had converted to a vineyard and Meg was travelling around wine-making regions learning the trade. She ended up here when I was about eight. My own mother had finally decided she wanted to live in Rome full-time and I hadn't seen her in months, and then there was this young woman who made it feel like the sun shone every time she smiled.'

Liv's face softened. 'You were smitten?'

'Totally. I worshipped her from the first day. She had this way of talking to me like I mattered, you know? Like I was more than just a kid. And by the end of that summer it was clear my dad was smitten too. He finalised the divorce from my mother and Meg stayed.' He stopped. It was impossible to express how his life had changed. How his father was so obviously happy and how that happiness made everything better, no more long silences, no more loneliness.

'It was Meg who encouraged me to paint, who persuaded my dad that a few years living and studying in Florence wouldn't mean the end of the Del Visconti dynasty. She never tried to be my mother, because I had one, distant though she was, but she was a friend and an aunt, and a big sister all rolled into one. I was eleven when Elisabetta came along and Meg spent a lot of time making sure I didn't feel excluded. And I didn't. Not once.'

'She sounds wonderful,' Liv said softly.

'She was. We were a family, Meg, Papa, Betta and I. I suppose I took it for granted, that security, that happiness.' He swallowed. 'That night I needed water, and when I got up my phone was flashing and I saw dozens of missed calls and messages. There had been an accident, their car had swerved off one of the mountain roads…' He heard Liv gasp. 'I needed to come immediately. And so I did. Looking back I think I disassociated from everything, my surroundings, the fact I wasn't alone, that you were there, that you even existed. I just needed to get to the hospital immediately.'

'That's completely understandable.'

'I didn't come out of that disassociation for weeks. My father and Meg had died instantly, they said. You know what came as a shock? The administration in the midst of grief.' He shook his head as he remembered. 'The Castello and the vineyards and the wine itself, the estates and the staff, all needing reassurance, continuity. The never-ending bureaucracy. And Elisabetta. In a coma at first, and then in need of surgery after surgery. Grieving and frightened and traumatised and only thirteen, still a child.'

'Oh Luciano.' Liv reached out and touched his arm. 'I am so sorry.'

'I couldn't think about anyone else. About before. I should have sent you a message at least. I knew I should, but I couldn't process why it mattered.'

'I don't think Elisabetta was the only one who was traumatised,' Liv murmured.

'I didn't even return to the apartment for several months. When I finally did, to pack up, you had left. I thought then about contacting you but so much time had passed I didn't know what to say. It was easier to put everything from before behind me. But it was wrong. I'm sorry.'

Liv didn't answer for a long time. 'I won't lie to you and pretend I didn't care,' she said at last. 'That I wasn't worried at first, and then upset, and then angry. I'm glad I know the truth, and I understand why it happened. So let's put it all in the past where it belongs and concentrate on getting through this wedding with our nerves intact.'

'Deal.'

'Okay then.' Liv got to her feet and looked around. 'So this is your memorial, for your father and Meg?'

'The churchyard was so overwhelming. I needed somewhere for Elisabetta that was peaceful, where she could be undisturbed. I needed it for me as well. Meg loved cherries, she would eat huge bowlfuls when they were in season, so the trees seemed fitting. The bench was carved by a friend of mine.'

Liv ran a hand along it. 'It's beautiful. And Elisabetta? How is she now?'

Luciano sighed. 'It took a long time. The surgeries and the rehabilitation, let alone the grief, readjusting to life with just me. Meg's family wanted her to move to New Zealand, to be with them, and honestly I thought it would be better for her too, but she was too sick to move at first and then she refused to go.' She'd imprinted on him like a motherless duckling, agitated whenever he was out of her sight. 'So in the end we agreed she should stay here. It's been hard for her, catching up educationally, socially, emotionally. She's seemed so much better but there are times like now when I realise how fragile she still is. I blame myself.' He stopped, shocked at how much he had said. Words and emotions he rarely admitted to himself, let alone third parties.

'Is that why she isn't here?"

'She wouldn't go to university, wouldn't travel, wouldn't do anything without me, so in a way I am glad she took this step. Just some, any notice would have been nice. A friend of hers has set up a yoga retreat in Thailand and Elisabetta headed off last minute to attend the opening, leaving just a note of apology and your brother's wedding to deal with. I think things got too much for her and she panicked and ran away.'

Liv nodded. 'Hence the need to keep the brides happy and the business viable. Well, I'll do what I can with this one and hopefully that buys you some time until she returns. Thank you for telling me, Luciano. I appreciate it. And I am so sorry. Meg sounds like a wonderful person. Thank you for the offer of dinner but I think I am going to try and sneak something to my room and get some sleep. See you around.'

And she was gone into the twilight, leaving Luciano alone with his memories. But for once they weren't just of his lost family but also of his time in Florence, and of the bright-eyed English girl he had met there.

# CHAPTER THREE

LIV LEANED AGAINST the archway which led to her room and thought longingly of the big comfortable bed just a staircase away. Every nerve, fibre, sinew and muscle was exhausted. She hadn't actually left the Castello grounds all day but according to her fitness tracker had clocked twenty thousand steps, many of them up and down stairs. At least she would be a great deal fitter at the end of this wedding.

*If* it ever ended. She half suspected she had accidentally ended up in Hades and rather than everlastingly push a boulder up a hill, her punishment for things unspecified was a never-ending to-do list and an increasingly irritable bride.

But on the other hand, at least being busy meant she didn't have too much time to think about the previous evening. She had got the answers she was seeking and the truth was far more heartbreaking than she could have imagined. She looked across at the round-turreted original Castello where she knew the family apartments went, her heart aching for Luciano and Elisabetta. What an unspeakable tragedy. No wonder Luciano was prepared to do whatever it took to keep his sister's business thriving in her unexpected absence.

She couldn't and didn't blame him for the way he had left her without a word. Not now. It was just… She stopped, grimacing at herself, wishing she wasn't being so brutally self-aware. It was just a bit of a jolt to realise he had forgotten her so easily then and subsequently. She had thought that night the start of something, that they meant something to each other, something that could endure no matter what. Now she knew the truth it would make the next week easier, but she would have to be careful not to spend too much time with Luciano. Because he was undeniably still more gorgeous, still had that same trick of looking a girl straight in the eye while he was talking and making her feel like she and only she was the sole focus of his attention, was still clearly intelligent and driven and successful and because despite everything, she still felt butterflies when he said her name in that deep, gravelly, accented voice.

Distance. Professionalism. Polite. She would continue to use her neutral smile on him too. She'd been using it so much it was practically stuck to her cheeks.

'Liv.' She jumped, startled out of her thoughts as Max hurried round the corner, his hair perfectly in place, his linen shorts and shirt once again perfectly ironed; how *did* he manage it? 'Here you are, Mum and Dad are almost here.'

*Here we go—don't talk about work, don't give anything away, avoid them as much as possible until the wedding is over and you have made a plan.* Liv tried to quell her panic by switching into details mode. 'The flowers are ready in their room, along with a welcome hamper of local produce, the same for the other bridesmaids when they arrive tomorrow.' Liv tried to visualise the spacious suite allotted to her parents. 'I think we have everything, robes, slippers, pool towels… I said flowers, didn't I?'

'What? Why are you worrying about flowers?'

Liv felt a jolt of annoyance at his surprise. Surely he knew that his fiancée had Liv, Francesca and any unfortunate staff member she could find at her beck and call as her demands escalated. The only comfort Liv could find was that Francesca was itemising every last-minute essential extra, ensuring there was a hefty service charge on top. 'Never mind that. You need to be there to greet them, come on.'

'I don't see why, it's not my wedding.' But Liv's protestations were ignored as Max pulled her round the front of the house where a car was heading up the driveway. Despite herself her heart hammered. Liv was determined not to mention her newly unemployed status this week but somehow her mother had the ability to read her mind. It was bad enough she was the only single one, right now the scruffy one as Max hadn't given her time to change. She really didn't want to be the only unemployed one as well.

The car drew up and first her parents and then her sister and Celeste, Portia's wife, got out of the car to be greeted with air kisses by Annabel, firm handshakes by Annabel's parents and hugs from Max. Liv hung back, aware of her denim shorts and dirty vest top, of her hair pulled back into a loose plait and her make-up-free face. She looked and felt like someone who had been on the go all day in the heat of an Italian summer. Her family in contrast didn't look as if they had just spent the day travelling; they all looked cool and composed and stylish, fitting exactly with Annabel's family aesthetic like the slightly sinister protagonists of a Netflix mini-series.

*Plot, a family wedding plunged into tragedy when the groom ran away and the staff revolted, tying the bride up with the many metres of discarded ribbon.* Liv started as she heard her name, trying to look attentive and promising herself to revisit the satisfying daydream later.

'…and Olivia will show you to your rooms so you can freshen up. We are meeting on the pool terrace for drinks. The owner of the house, Luciano Del Visconti, has invited us to a wine tasting and dinner tonight, while we are still just immediate family.' Annabel looked around, her smile slipping as she spotted Liv.

'Oh, good, Olivia. There you are.'

'Mum, Dad. Portia, Celeste.' Liv embraced and was embraced by each family member in turn. 'I hope you had a good journey?'

'Darling,' her dad said as he pulled her in for a hug. 'Not bad, thank you. This is quite the place, isn't it?'

'Olivia.' Her mother surveyed her up and

down. 'Look at your top, it's filthy, what *have* you been doing?'

'Liv has been a huge help.' Her brother put a reassuring hand on her shoulder. He knew how easily her mother's criticism got to Liv. 'Annabel would be in bits without her, wouldn't you, pumpkin?'

'I wouldn't say *bits*,' Annabel protested.

'I've been more than happy to help. Come on, I'll show you to your rooms. Max, can you help with luggage? I'll point out the pool area as well, so you know where to go afterwards.' She stepped back and smiled at her brother. 'Actually, Max,' she said quietly, trying to keep her voice casual, 'I was thinking I might just grab some food and eat in my room again tonight. Those table changes Annabel wants mean relooking at the whole plan and…'

'Absolutely not.' Max flung an arm around her shoulders and squeezed. 'I appreciate you helping, Liv, but you are here as my sister not as a wedding planner. Come drink wine and celebrate with me.'

'I do hope you have something more suitable to wear,' her mother interjected. 'Really, Olivia, you look like you are the one who spent all day on a plane.'

*Neutral smile.* 'Nope, just spent all day

running around a huge Italian castle. Okay, this way.'

With Max and a couple of castle staff taking care of the bags Liv repeated the quick tour she had received yesterday, pointing out the path to the pool, the kitchen and relaxing spaces before finally depositing the two couples into their rooms. Her parents and sister had been allotted beautiful suites complete with sitting rooms, both three times the size of her courtyard room with their high ceilings and huge windows. Not that she would swap the rustic charm and little balcony she was growing to love for these more palatial spaces even without the inducement of a courtyard separating her from her family.

'Okay,' she said after Portia and Celeste were settled in their room and her mother had pronounced her rooms acceptable. 'I'll leave you to settle in. As you can see, I am in need of a shower myself so…' She backed towards the door.

'Wait a moment,' her mother commanded and Liv stopped. She was proud of her mother and all she had achieved, but she did hate it when her mother used her judge voice on her as if Liv was a misbehaving barrister and not her daughter. ‘Olivia, why exactly are you rushing around like a paid member of staff?’

‘There have been a few language-barrier issues, so I volunteered to help and ensure the wedding goes well. Turns out my year in Italy did have some uses after all.’ Her decision to study Italian and art history at a small coastal university had been treated with a mixture of surprise and amused contempt by a family who specialised in law at Oxbridge.

‘Hmm.’ Her mother looked unconvinced. ‘It seems to me that you have been very elusive recently. This isn’t an excuse not to spend time with us, is it? I know you don’t want to talk about the future, darling, but you have to face facts. If you don’t make partner soon all those ambitious early twenty-somethings will start to overtake you. You’ll be thirty soon and you really need to be more strategic. I think that we should take advantage of us all being together to have a family summit and help you formulate a plan, to try and get you back on the right path.’

The right path to her mother meant the conventional path, high-powered career and moneymaking path, the settling-down path. In some ways she was very open-minded. She hadn’t blinked when Portia introduced Celeste as her fiancée and had embraced the latter as a daughter. In fact, Liv often thought that she preferred the elegant Frenchwoman to her actual youngest daughter, but both women had professional jobs, a beautiful home and were considering a family. All ticks on the Clara Davenport guide to a respectable life.

Liv had tried to follow her mother's template but she had stopped pretending it made her happy. Her law conversion had been stultifyingly dull and her job even more so. She had hated the expectation that she lived to work, the demanding hours, the competitive presenteeism, the stress of every second being billable, felt like she was losing herself in the never-ending pressure to perform. In the end she had stopped performing, started to prioritise her weekly art class, to take her annual leave and not check her emails religiously while she was away, all of which had led to last week's meeting and six months' salary in lieu of notice or putting up a fuss. All of which meant she did need to regroup—her mother was right there—but not in any direction her mother meant.

'No need for a summit, I am fine,' she said as convincingly as she could. 'And this is Annabel and Max's occasion, they need to be the centre of attention, not me. But you're right, this shirt *is* disgusting, I've been hauling bits of furniture around and it shows, so let me shower and change and I'll see you at the pool, okay?' There was no way she could get away with not coming to dinner, not with her mother zeroing in so quickly. Which meant worlds colliding in ways she was really not comfortable with.

Aware that she was under scrutiny Liv took a little longer over changing than she had intended. At least, she told herself it was for that reason. Why else would she brush her strawberry blonde hair until it gleamed, using the curling tongs to add a little bounce into the poker-straight strands? Why else would she take her time getting her eyeliner just so and mess around with bronzer and highlighter before wiping it all away for her usual light application of tinted moisturiser, mascara and lip tint? Why did she spend ten minutes staring at her outfits, discarding every choice before choosing a summery yellow maxi dress which nipped in at the waist and added some pleasing curves to her figure?

Obviously, this extra care wasn't for Luciano; that would be absurd. Whatever she had thought was blossoming between them eight years ago had been in her imagination. She had been a one-night stand on the eve of the worst night of his life, nothing more, nothing less. And her family must never guess that there had ever been anything, no matter how illusory, between them.

Finally, she was ready and could put off dinner no longer. Taking a deep breath to try to quell the flock of butterflies that had decided to make a home in her stomach, Liv reluctantly stepped out of her room and made her way to the courtyard. She cast a longing look towards the house and for one moment considered sneaking into the kitchen, grabbing some food and retreating, before tilting her chin and marching onwards. Was she a mouse or a Davenport? She had nothing to be ashamed of. But despite her resolve her steps faltered as she reached the pool. The large stone terrace looked inviting, flanked with large plant-filled pots and dotted around with tables and chairs, lights carefully positioned to give the whole a wonderland quality. The pool itself was smooth and blue and, in the warm evening air, inviting. Liv gave it a longing glance before heading over to the assembled group. The other bridesmaids were due to arrive the next day but for now it was just immediate family and, she realised, they were all in couples. Annabel glowed as she whispered something in Max's ear which made her brother laugh. Celeste and Portia were in conversation with Annabel's parents, and her own parents were… Oh goodness, they were talking to Luciano.

She hovered for one moment, feeling on the outside, all her poise deserting her. How could she help lead contract negotiations with a team of international lawyers or present her case to a judge but be at a loss when confronted with those who were supposed to love her unconditionally? For one moment her resolve broke and she took a step backwards, but Max looked up and saw her and waved her over.

'Liv, at last! You don't want to miss the wine tasting Luciano has laid on.'

'No,' she agreed, neutral smile firmly back on her mouth. 'I definitely don't want to do that.'

Not that she would be partaking of much. Tempting as the thought of sinking into a large glass or two was, Liv needed all her wits about her.

It was no surprise that Luciano was a good host. He had always been charming with a keen sense of humour, and the wedding party were soon gathered around the table set up for wine tasting, hanging on his every word as they tried an assortment of delicious local wines, most made by the Casa Del Visconti. Liv made sure to make good use of the spittoon but not everyone followed her example and even though the servings were tasting size only, many of the group were on the jolly side of tipsy when they sat down to the meal Luciano had organised. The huge bowls of salads, freshly baked breads, grilled fish, meats and vegetables looked and smelt amazing but Liv had little appetite. It was like one of her dreams had come true, only in a twisted, nightmarish way. There were ten at the table, four couples and her and Luciano, but she was acting as if she barely knew him, as if they had met for the first time yesterday. But there had been times during the year of their friendship, times when she had hoped friendship was developing into something more, that she had imagined this exact scenario. Imagined bringing Luciano home, introducing him to her parents and siblings. They would have liked him, approved. She winced. It was always embarrassing to realise just how much her family's approval mattered for all she told herself it didn't.

The salads were replaced with fresh berries and an array of delicate small cakes. More wine was poured, along with strong aromatic coffee and the large group broke up. Annabel and Max headed off for a walk, hand in hand, and Annabel's parents excused themselves; they were collecting family from the airport in Pisa the next day and had an early start.

Liv half expected Luciano to also make his excuses and leave, but he remained lounging at the head of the table, wine glass in hand, charming her parents and sister. Liv took little part in the conversation, but she was aware of his eyes on her on more than one occasion, a quizzical, faintly troubled expression in his eyes.

Liv was just considering slipping away when Max returned without Annabel, who had decided to also get an early night, and he sat back down next to Luciano. Before long Max, Luciano, Liv's father and Celeste were enthusiastically discussing Italian football, leaving Liv at the mercy of her mother and sister. There was no escaping now, the attempt she made instantly foiled.

'It's still early,' her mother said as Liv muttered something about a good night's sleep sounding like a good idea. 'And darling, we have hardly seen you. You have been even more elusive the last few months than usual.'

'Not elusive, Mum, just busy.'

'We're all busy, Olivia. Look at your sister, full-time job, exploring IVF, on two boards, running marathons and she still finds time to call me twice a week and come for Sunday dinner once a month.'

Liv couldn't help but look at her sister, poised, elegant, successful.

'I was sorry to hear that you and Josh broke up,' Portia said.

Was it Liv's imagination, or did Luciano look over at the mention of Josh's name?

'We didn't break up exactly, after all we were hardly dating,' Liv protested uncomfortably. She should have known better than to agree to a date with her sister's colleague in the first place; she preferred her private life to be exactly that. Private.

'I was surprised when he asked for your details after that conference, you're not his usual type at all. I hope you weren't too upset it didn't work out.'

Liv picked up her glass and took a large gulp, resolutions to keep her wits about her discarded. 'Actually, I was the one who broke things off with him.' Her only regret was doing so after six dates, not straight away but she had vowed to try to give the men she dated a chance, aware that she was prone to walk away over the slightest detail. Walk out before she was walked out on. She flicked a quick glance at Luciano, she didn't need a psychology degree to figure out where that behaviour came from.

'*You* did?' It wasn't often her sister was at a loss for words and Liv enjoyed the way she spluttered to a stop, the incredulity that spread over her face. Although why should she be so incredulous? Josh had been nice looking, had a good job, owned a swanky waterfront flat but he was also hilariously self-absorbed, more than a little vain and rude to waiters. He was no loss.

'He wasn't my type.'

'Darling,' her mother said. 'You are nearly thirty. You need to be a little less picky, all the good ones are being snapped up, you know.'

Oh, this was *excruciating* and she was sure Luciano was listening. Liv's hand tightened on the stem of her glass,

'It's not picky to decide against dating

someone who summons waiters with a click of his fingers.'

'If you want to settle down…'

'Who says I *want* to settle down? There are more ways to be happy than marriage and kids and paying off a mortgage. Maybe I want to do something different. Take a gap year, travel. Volunteer. See the world.'

But her impassioned independence speech made no impact on her mother.

'Olivia, we all have to grow up sometime. What about your job? Any sign of a partnership there? Do you want me to talk to Lionel? We trained together, you know.'

Portia leaned across the table. 'I heard that there are going to be some efficiencies at Campion, Marple and Wimsey. They don't impact you, do they? This is why it's always good to be seen to be on the fast track, they won't risk losing future partners to other firms.'

Liv swallowed. This was the last conversation she wanted to have. Unwillingly she remembered the meeting just last week, the pity in her boss's eyes, the reminder that everyone needed to contribute to the bottom line, that every minute not billed impacted on the firm, that examples needed to be set and the right to a work-life balance earned.

'Well, I...' Liv stopped. She couldn't lie outright but nor could she admit the truth, confirming her family's suspicions that in their opinion she wasn't fit to manage her own life, no matter that she had been doing exactly that for the past eleven years. 'I...'

Luciano didn't mean to eavesdrop. Liv's unexpected arrival at his home, the memories she evoked with every word and movement were a shock, an opening of the Pandora's box titled Before he kept locked and put away. A box he was determined to keep locked away. He was a different person now. The tragedies and losses of the past eight years had changed him; they'd had to. In one night his carefree world had disappeared, his freedom to follow his passions. He'd had to step up into a parenting role for an injured, grieving child, take on responsibilities at home and work he had been in no way prepared for. Had he succeeded? Last week he would have said an unequivocal yes. This week, however, Elisabetta's absence weighing heavily and the stirring up of old memories made it a much more difficult question.

He might have succeeded in carrying on, but was he happy? That wasn't a question he ever allowed himself to consider. He dated, a little, but never seriously, unable to give his romantic life the time and commitment it needed; prioritising himself felt self-indulgent. It wasn't something he thought he regretted, but seeing Liv again made him wonder if he was just very good at lying to himself.

But he was happier than Liv was right now, her cheeks flushed with indignation or humiliation, her hand wrapped tightly around her rapidly emptying wine glass, her eyes half closed, like a child trying to block reality out as her mother and sister scolded her in tandem. He noticed her father and brother glance towards her, concern in their eyes, but neither made a move to intervene.

'I'm sorry to interrupt,' he lied, getting to his feet. 'But I believe I promised you a moonlit tour of the vineyard, Liv. The stars are very clear tonight, which make the conditions perfect.'

He winced internally at the speculative glances her family shot at the two of them, the amused smile on Celeste's face.

'Stars,' Liv repeated, a little bemused, then straightened, understanding and then relief evident on her always expressive face. 'Yes, of course. Great!'

'Please,' he said to her family. 'Stay here as long as you would like. Drink some more wine, ask my staff if you need anything at all.' He gestured to a path that led from the terrace back to the house. 'Liv, if you're ready, this way.'

Liv fell in beside him as he made his way into the courtyard, her mouth curved into a complicit smile. 'I must have a very bad memory, I don't remember anything about a moonlit tour.'

'It seemed to me that you might appreciate rescuing back there.'

She bit her lip. 'That obvious?'

'Only if you know the signs. My sister's relations, on her mother's side. They can be…' He sought for the right words. 'They love her and care about her, but they don't understand her and that can seem like disapproval.'

'Yes, that's it exactly. I don't doubt, I have never doubted that they love me, that they only want what's best for me. The problem is they think they know what that is better than I ever could, that without their guidance I will fail.' She laughed then, low and musical, the sound transporting him back a decade to other sultry summer evenings. 'Did you see their faces?

They all obviously thought this was some kind of assignation.'

'Assignation?'

'Moonlit tour and stargazing just the two of us? Luciano, my parents think we are on a date.'

'I couldn't think of anything else plausible this late,' he started to explain, and Liv laughed again.

'First, they have to deal with the realisation that I dumped Josh, not the other way round. Now they think I am being whisked away on a romantic walk by the rich, handsome owner of an Italian castle. My stock has never been higher. Maybe I'll tell them about my job after all. Hopefully they will be so distracted by the size of your turrets they won't be too disappointed that I'll be job-hunting again.'

'Your sister was right, your role has been cut?' An idea occurred to him. She was working well with Francesca, in one day had made sense of Elisabetta's system, or lack of one, and was showing remarkable patience with the bride. If she needed a job and he needed a temp…

It made sense but was it wise considering their shared history?

'Long story and it's late. Thank you, Luciano. For the rescue and for shocking my entire family into silence…'

'Why?'

'Why what?'

'Why would they be shocked if I was whisking you away on a pre-arranged assignation? You are funny and smart and beautiful. I would be lucky if you agreed to accompany me.'

Their eyes caught, held, and Luciano could feel his blood thundering through his veins. Why had he said that? He had unwittingly hurt Liv Davenport once before and he was in no place for anything romantic now, not with a busy summer and his continual worry about Elisabetta to deal with.

And yet he couldn't help wishing that he had the mental space to enjoy the stars with a beautiful woman he was attracted to, that he hadn't hurt Liv in the past, that this could be the assignation her family imagined.

'That's…' Her voice was husky. 'That's really nice of you to say.'

'I'm not being nice, I am being truthful.' He should step away, walk away, stop holding her gaze, stop noticing how her pupils were dilated and how her hair waved around her face and how full and inviting her mouth was. 'I don't know how you don't see what I see.'

'The woman who is saving your staff from an overstressed bride-to-be?'

'That's just a very small part of it.' It was unreasonable to expect Liv to be the same as she had been eight years ago. After all, look how *he* had changed. But she had been so sure of herself back then, her excitement at living in the ancient city shining through, her enthusiasm for the art on every corner palpable. He still saw glimpses of that Liv, especially when she was running around, a list in one hand, pieces of ribbon in the other, but it spluttered and died in the presence of her family.

'Anyway, thanks for the rescue, I really appreciate it.' Liv shifted, clearly uncomfortable with the compliment. 'This is me…' she gestured towards the door to one of the courtyard rooms. 'So, I'll head up. It's been a long day.' But although she stopped she made no move to head up the stairs, turning to face him instead.

'We could actually *go* stargazing. It's a clear night so should be spectacular.' Luciano had had no intention of following through with the actual walk. Things felt unsteady already, thanks to Elisabetta's absence and the stirring of old memories. But Liv's face was luminescent in the moonlight, her eyes huge and all he knew was he didn't want to say goodnight yet.

'I really should head up, it's been a busy day and tomorrow looks even more so.' Liv grimaced. 'Listen to me. I really don't *need* to do anything. I am on holiday, and yet I have spent the last thirty hours as Annabel's personal wedding planner, and the last hour subjected to a family interrogation. I deserve a walk, even if…'

'Even if what?'

'It's not the most sensible idea I have ever had.'

Luciano didn't need to ask any more questions. He knew why spending time together in the moonlit evening wasn't wise. Knew that she too felt the pull of those younger selves who thought they had all the time in the world to flirt and tease and fall towards something that might have made it to love if fate hadn't intervened.

'I don't know about you, but I spend my whole life being sensible,' he said and she laughed.

'Me too, but I have made a vow to live more spontaneously, to try new things.'

'Then a walk it is. If the *bella donna* would like to follow me…' Wisdom be damned.

The stars were shining, there was a beautiful woman by his side. What red-blooded Italian man could resist?

# CHAPTER FOUR

So much for keeping her distance from Luciano! But if Liv's options were listening to her mother telling her what a failure she was, sitting alone in her room on this beautiful sultry summer night or taking an ill-advised walk with the man who had come perilously close to breaking her heart there was only one option. She obediently followed Luciano as he took her through the gardens along a path faintly lit by low solar lanterns.

'There's a sky park not far from here which is spectacular,' Luciano said. 'I used to take Elisabetta there when she couldn't sleep, but it's quite a drive, so I installed a hut on the top of this hill so she could just come to see the stars here no matter what the weather, although there's no need for it on a night like this.'

'You sound like an amazing brother.'

He shook his head. 'I operated on instinct,

mostly just muddled my way through. I think I mentioned that her mother's family wanted to take her back to New Zealand, thought she needed routine and structure and normality not stargazing huts. It got messy for a while, a lot of pressure on me to force her into a move until they accepted that she wanted to stay here.' He shook his head. 'I don't know, sometimes I think maybe they were right. She seems fine for a while but when things overwhelm her, she can't cope, as you are all too aware.'

'Still, she's done an amazing job building up the wedding business even if her filing leaves a lot to be desired. How long has she been doing it?'

'Three years. She didn't want to go to university, to travel, to do anything when she finished at school, she just wanted to work here. We already hosted walking and vineyard tours, part of Meg's initiatives, corporate events. Like mother like daughter, I suppose, Elisabetta had a real knack for the people and events side and she had been suggesting weddings for a few years. That first year was just a couple of late bookings, last year we had six and this year it really took off. We have already hosted several late spring and early summer and are fully booked right up to harvest. It's a huge change, which is why she got overwhelmed. I just wish she'd spoken to me, rather than running away.' The frustration and pain in his voice was palpable and Liv's heart ached for him.

'Did you say she didn't give you any warning?'

'Just a note and a text from the airport.'

'Ouch.'

'Her mother's family would say it's just another example of how spoiled she is,' he said ruefully. 'Maybe they are right. I went with what she said she needed, what felt right, but what did I know? Like I said, I often wonder if I should have sent her to them.'

'Maybe, but she might have felt abandoned and unwanted, exiled from her home and her memories of before. It might have worked out or she might have been bitter and resentful. She's still very young and she's been through a lot. I don't mean she should just abandon her responsibilities with no consequences but actually she was right this is a great place for weddings and the setup she has put in place is pretty good, but to go from a handful to being fully booked would faze someone with a lot more experience than she has.'

'Would it faze you?' There was a strange intensity to Luciano's voice, and he was looking at Liv as if her answer really mattered.

'After six years in corporate law hell not much fazes me,' she said and then stopped still. 'Oh, my goodness! Look at that! I have never seen so many stars!' Liv gazed up in awe. As they had rounded the hill the lights from the Castello had faded away, the last of the solar lights just out of view, but she didn't need to worry about misstepping. The moon was only a quarter full but low and cast just enough of a silvery light for her to pick her way, amplified by what seemed like millions of stars. Wordlessly Luciano guided her to a bench and she sank back, still looking upward. It was as if the stars were putting on a carnival just for her, dancing and wheeling and shining with an intensity that made her dizzy.

'I have never seen anything so beautiful,' she murmured at last, not sure if one second, minute or hour had passed. The timelessness of the stars made her own concerns seem petty; she had never felt so small, so insignificant and yet so aware of her role in the vast universe. 'None of it really matters, does it? Money, status, all that counts is doing your best.' It was what she had always believed, that being true to herself mattered, but she had lost that clarity along the way, had opted for fitting in rather than walking alone. No more, she vowed to the stars. She was glad she had the opportunity to make a new start and if she made some missteps along the way that was fine.

Slowly she came back to the here and now, uncomfortably aware that Luciano wasn't studying the night sky but that he was looking at her, a thoughtful expression on his face.

'What? Have I got something in my hair?' Liv brushed a lock back self-consciously.

'No, not at all. I was just thinking how right it feels that our paths connected once again.'

'Because I saved you from Annabel?'

'Partly.'

Liv was both desperate for him to continue and for him to stop. She knew what he meant. Within just one day they had fallen into their old companionship, the conversation going far deeper than the surface reminiscences of old acquaintances. How quickly and easily they had slipped back into their old intimacy. In some ways it was as if the intervening years, the disappearance hadn't happened.

Acquaintances were all they could be. They couldn't return to that old *would they wouldn't they* dance. She might understand his reasons for disappearing that night, for not contacting her afterwards but once ghosted twice shy. And they were different people now: he was no longer an impassioned, talented artist but a businessman with huge responsibilities, and she was at a crossroads.

So, it would be super helpful if he stopped looking at her like that.

Worse, she suspected she was looking at him in exactly the same way.

Because it couldn't be denied that Luciano Del Visconti was a very handsome man. Nor could it be denied that she had thought about that night once or twice in the last eight years, more. That no other man had ever measured up, not that there had been many, thanks to that habit of hers of walking away first.

Oh no, had she swayed towards him? It was as if Liv had no control of her body, of her breath, which hitched as she moistened her suddenly dry lips.

'Liv?' His voice was low, a caress.

'Yes?'

'If your job has let you go and you don't have any plans, then would you consider staying for the rest of the summer?'

What? 'Staying here?' With Luciano? Her

heart sped up. Did he mean he wanted to get to know her again, to rekindle what had been cut short all those years ago? Surely not, and yet hadn't she just been thinking how easily they had fallen into that old intimacy?

'I need someone to run these weddings. Even if Elisabetta comes home sooner than anticipated, she will need support. You are good with details, the staff like you, your job situation is complicated, you are bilingual. You are perfect.'

Liv sat back, her cheeks hot with humiliation. 'A job?' Was that her voice? So unnaturally high? How on earth had she got the situation so wrong? There she was, thinking Luciano was going to kiss her and instead he what? Felt sorry for her? 'I'm not a professional events planner. Besides, my home is in London.'

'I can offer you bed and board as well as a generous wage. Forgive me if I am overstepping but it seems to me you are looking for new challenges. This could give you the time to plan your next step. Even if Elisabetta came home tomorrow I wouldn't want her resuming full-time work. In fact I am sure I don't. I'm glad she's finally left home, I want to encourage her to travel more and to make sure she has the space to do so whilst supporting her to continue to build on what she has here.'

*It seems to me you are looking for new challenges.* How had he surmised that from a handful of conversations and the way she had tried to elude her sister's questions?

'I am looking for a next step, that's true. But I can't just stay here.'

'Why not?'

'Because…' Because what? She didn't need to work her notice, no one was expecting her at work on Monday. She had no pets, no plants that relied on her even, her every attempt to fill her home with greenery ending in brown leaf disaster. Her pay-off would hit her bank account in a few weeks, enough to pay her bills and mortgage for a year, and if she preferred it would be easy to let her flat. 'You can't offer me a job based on a couple of days helping out.'

'I've seen more than enough to know you would be a good fit. I'd need you until the end of October. We have a couple of autumn weddings and several vineyard and walking tours booked in then.'

Until the end of October? That would give her four months to figure out what next. Retrain, maybe mediation, less adversarial but still using her hard-won legal skills. Or maybe she could look right back to her degree, to her love of art and languages. Or travel. See the world, see where the wind took her. The possibilities were endless.

Liv tilted her head back and looked at the stars, still dancing above her. The words she had spoken at dinner echoed through her head. She *could* travel. There was so much out there, temples and museums and places of incredible natural beauty and she had seen so little of it.

Saying yes would give her options. But it would also mean living with Luciano for four months. And for all she told herself anything she had ever felt for him was in the past, her star-addled reaction to him earlier showed she was very much still susceptible to his charm—and she'd only been here just over twenty-four hours! On the other hand, that attraction was clearly only one-way; while she had been thinking romance he had been thinking job offers. She needed to take a step back, think about this logically, away from the stars and the embarrassment of crossed wires.

'I would need to think about it,' she said, aware she had kept him hanging for an answer much longer than was polite. 'Can I let you know before the end of the week?'

'Of course.'

'Thank you for bringing me here, it's beautiful.' She paused, gathered up her courage for what she needed to say. 'But Luciano, I don't need rescuing. I have been handling my parents for a long time. I know they love me. They just worry about me. They see beauty in security, in savings and pensions and marriage, in ambition and achievements. My mother is a judge, my father one of the most well known barristers in the country, and Portia is following in his footsteps. Max is the kind of corporate lawyer I can never be and Celeste heads up a charity. They want me to fly as high as they do, because to them that means happiness.'

'And what does happiness mean to you, Liv?'

She allowed herself to turn to look at him, just briefly, to take in the slant of his cheek, the curve of his mouth, to feel the tug towards him one more time, and then she stood up, feelings locked away. 'Freedom,' she said. 'To choose my own path, to own my decisions. That's what I want. Thank you for bringing me here, it's beautiful. And thank you for the offer. I will consider it, I promise. We'd better get back before my mother starts planning our wedding.'

And without another glance at the star-filled sky she turned and headed back to the Castello and her family, leaving Luciano motionless on the bench behind her.

Host duties done, Luciano resolved to see as little of the Davenport–Anstruther-Jones party as possible. Apart from anything else he had been aware of the speculative gleams in parental and sibling eyes when he had asked Liv to walk with him and he didn't want to encourage questions or gossip. But they were hard to avoid. Some weddings, he had learned over the last two years, were contained. A few days of close friends and family celebrating together. Others seemed to permeate every corner of the castle. This was very much the latter. Every day there were more and more people. First the bridesmaids and the rest of the bride's immediate family, then wider family from both sides, then friends complete with plus ones. But no children. This was very much a child-free zone. Pity, Luciano enjoyed the element of chaos children brought to a wedding. If he ever... He stopped, his laptop a blur as he pushed his chair back and jumped to his feet.

If he ever married. It was a sobering thought. To get married one needed to be in a long-term relationship. Luciano had achieved many things over the last eight years but that particular path had eluded him. He was too busy, often needing to cancel dates at the last moment, unable to commit to future plans. Even when he *was* there, one girlfriend had complained bitterly, he was only ever *half* there. He had had no defence against her comment. Elisabetta came first, work second, his personal life a very distant, mostly forgotten third.

The truth was work was easy to bury himself in; relationships were a different matter. The last time he had truly lost himself in another person was, well, it was with Liv. So no wonder he was so discombobulated by this particular wedding, these particular guests. They brought the past back, brought Liv with her bright eyes and bright smile and bright face always within sight or so it seemed, chatting to one of his team, never-ending list in hand. He swore he could smell her perfume wherever he walked, hear her laugh echo in every corner, that memory of the night on the hillside playing over and over again.

He had so nearly kissed her under the stars,

aching to taste her once again, to hold her, to relearn her. Instead he had offered her a job.

He didn't know which was more foolhardy.

His watch buzzed, notifying him of a message and Luciano reached for his phone, smiling as he opened the selfie Elisabetta had sent him. She already looked more relaxed. It was only with hindsight that he could see how drawn she had been, how dark the shadows under her eyes. A typed message appeared under the photo.

Miss me?

Not at all. But wish I was there.

Luc it is heavenly. I wish I could stay here forever.

A pause and then…

I am sorry for just leaving. It was selfish. Don't worry, I'll be back next week.

Back next week? In that case they could muddle through. No need for a temp, no need for Liv to delay her plans, by next week the past could be locked firmly away where it belonged out of sight and hopefully out of mind.

Luciano sighed and took another look at the picture his sister had sent of herself, cross-legged on the beach, smiling, relaxed, young and alive and vibrant.

Happy.

You don't have to hurry back, when did you last take any time off? While you are over there why not see something of the country? Go to Cambodia, Vietnam? You could even head over to New Zealand afterwards.

He pressed Send and almost immediately his phone rang. With a wry grin he answered and was instantly greeted by his sister's voice.

'Luciano Del Visconti, are you trying to sack me?'

'Good morning, *cara*. Or is it evening where you are?'

'Don't change the subject. What do you mean stay out here? Look, I know I dropped you well and truly in it and I shouldn't have just taken off…'

Luciano interrupted, knowing just how lengthy an apology from Elisabetta could be. 'No. You shouldn't. You should have spoken to me and saved us both a lot of unnecessary angst. But, Betta.' He closed his eyes and thought of Liv. Of the way her face dimmed when she was caught under the weight of her family's expectations. Love could be a burden sometimes, stifle where it was meant to nourish. 'You went straight from school to working here, you have never travelled, you didn't go to university. How do you know the vineyard is what you truly want rather than all you really know? You deserve some time out to discover that, to discover you.'

'I had plenty of self-reflection time when I was a teen.'

'Operations and convalescence aren't the same as real time out. Betta, you barely spend your wages, you must have enough stashed away to fund a few months' travel.'

A long pause and then a faintly sulky 'I guess.'

'So live a little, spend a little. See the world, go visit your family.'

'Why are you always trying to send me to New Zealand when you know they…?'

'When they want what's best for you and always have? Your mother's family love you. Besides you are their link to her. You might actually enjoy spending time with them. They will have so many stories and pictures that will be new to you.'

'I guess, but what about the weddings? There's the rest of the season and we get enquiries for the next few years all the time.'

'I'll get someone in.' The more he thought about it the more he realised sending his sister away was the best thing for both of them. They were so defined by the tragedy that had changed their lives, it would do her good to get out in the world. '*Cara*, if you spend some time away and realise this is exactly where you want to be, then that's wonderful. If you decide it isn't, then that's fine too, this will always be your home. But you need to know what your alternatives are. I sometimes wonder if I should have pushed harder for you to go to university.'

His sister laughed, but when she spoke her voice was soft. 'One of the many things I love about you is that you don't push me at all. You just pointed out the consequences if I didn't do my physio or have another operation and let me make up my own mind.'

Luciano could feel his throat thicken. 'We muddled along somehow, didn't we?'

'We did more than that. I know how much you gave up for me. I don't want you to ever think I am not grateful.'

'I don't need you to be grateful,' Luciano said quickly. 'Just happy.'

'Right back at you. You know what I would love?'

'Your own yoga centre here?'

'Actually yes but no. For you to paint again.'

'For me to *what*?' He froze as she continued.

'When I was growing up you were always covered in paint. I still have the mural you did in my room, I never want it painted over. And I love that picture you did as a wedding present for Mama and Papa, the one of the Castello? I know they did too.'

He winced. 'I was a child, the proportions are all over the place.'

'No, it's beautiful, you were so talented. I just wish you hadn't stopped, that's all.'

Luciano stared out of the window. People had wondered if he would be jealous when Elisabetta was born but he hadn't been. Partly because his father and Meg had made sure he was always included, partly because he had loved Elisabetta the moment he had met the solemn-eyed baby and partly because now he was no longer the sole Del Visconti heir, her very existence gave him freedom.

But he hadn't been able to escape his destiny for long.

'Painting, the way I did, wasn't something I could fit in around other responsibilities. It was all-or-nothing.' He closed his eyes, remembering the way time would evaporate, aware of nothing but the brush in his hand. It felt so real, he could smell the paint, see the colours, feel the texture of the brush in his hand, and for the first time in a long, long time allowed himself to acknowledge how empty he sometimes felt. He enjoyed his work, was good at it, but it didn't nourish his soul.

'Maybe I'll decide that what I want is your job and then you will be free to do whatever you want.'

'Maybe. But, Betta. Don't think I have any regrets. I did what had to be done, but I wanted to. Raising you, taking over the estates, the vineyards. None of it was a sacrifice and you don't owe me anything. So take the time while you can. You've earned it.'

'I love you, big brother.'

'I love you too. Now, tell me all about what you've been up to.' Luciano settled down to listen to his sister as she took him through the last few days in exhaustive detail. She was alive, she was healthy, she sounded happy.

It was all he had ever wanted. But if Elisabetta was ready to spread her wings, where did that leave him? Was it time for him to start to branch out too, terrifying as that thought was? What did that even look like, practically, emotionally? With Liv's reappearance in his life, was he ready for further changes, especially if she took him up on his job offer and they occupied the same space for the next few months? He pushed the thought away for another day. He had the rest of his life to figure that out after all.

Luciano didn't set out to find Liv but, as so often seemed to happen these days, his path led inexorably straight to her. Which, considering he ended up in the walled garden where the wedding would take place the next day, wasn't that surprising. She was standing, hands on hips, watching the ribbon, in the right shade at last, get tied around the sixty chairs lined up in neat rows facing the pretty pergola where the ceremony would take place. Her hair was pulled back into a loose knot and her face make-up free, dusted with that smattering of freckles that made her look younger than her twenty-nine years. She wore her usual working uniform of denim shorts and a vest top, her eyes hidden by her sunglasses. She looked beautiful and once again Luciano was haunted by memories, not just of Florence but the other night. The night when she was so close, when he'd nearly kissed her only to remember all the reasons he shouldn't and offered her a job instead.

'It's looking good,' he said as he neared, and she grimaced.

'Good will not be enough. It has to be perfect.'

'Where are the happy couple?'

'Max is at the airport picking up the last of the relatives. Annabel and her bridesmaids have gone to a spa to ready themselves for tomorrow. My parents, sister and Celeste are on an improving day in Florence. Which gives me some space to get things done.'

'Liv, this is meant to be a favour for your brother not a vocation. You should be at the spa or in Florence, you know the city better than any of your family.'

He tried to remember if any of her relatives had visited her the year she spent there but he didn't think so. But he did know how she loved to explore the city, to find new alleyways and squares, to hunt out small ristorantes off the beaten track.

'Actually, maybe this is a vocation, or an audition at least. To see if I want to take you up on your offer and stay here for the summer. If you meant it, that is?' She looked up at him in query.

'I just spoke to my sister.'

'That's brilliant, how was she?'

'Brighter, better, so much so this time away is clearly what she needed so I have suggested she stays out there, travels a little.'

'So you definitely need someone.'

'I really do.'

'Situation still desperate enough that a failed lawyer will do?'

'Situation desperate enough that only a bilingual lawyer on hiatus who miraculously can make sense of my sister's idiosyncratic filing system will do.'

Liv bit her lip and then stuck out her hand. 'In that case you have a deal.'

Luciano took her warm hand in his, struck by the feel of her skin on his. 'Welcome to the Castello Del Visconti. I look forward to working with you.'

He let go of her hand but his palm and fingers were still warm, still tingled where he had touched her and it was all he could do not to reach out and touch her again. As he turned to go, Luciano hoped he wasn't making a mistake offering Liv the opportunity to stay. He couldn't deny he was still attracted to her and at times he thought she might reciprocate that attraction, not that he deserved it if she did. But not only would he be her boss but he was still unsure what the future held for him, had spent so long locking his feelings away he wasn't sure he was able to free them. He might be ready to start contemplating what his future might hold, even think about relationships, but he couldn't experiment with Liv; she deserved better. He had hurt her once and he needed to make sure he never had the opportunity to do so again; that way they would both be safe.

# CHAPTER FIVE

'I CAN'T BELIEVE my favourite brother is married!' Liv smiled up at Max as they swayed together in the middle of the dance floor, occasionally in time with the music.

'Your *only* brother,' Max pointed out. He looked so handsome in his light grey suit, his eyes alight with happiness.

'Which makes you my favourite, although you were edged out by Fluffy for a while.'

'Fluffy?'

'My imaginary dog.'

Max let out a shout of laughter. 'How could I forget Fluffy? You insisted on having a place in the car for him and a blanket at the bottom of the bed. You really were the cutest kid. Weird but cute, head full of stories and imagination.'

'Oh, it still is,' Liv confided. 'Only I hide it better now.'

'There's little space for imagination in contract law.'

'True.' She was not going to ruin Max's day by telling him about her change in employment, although she needed to come clean soon. She would be returning to London the day after tomorrow with the rest of the family, but only for less than twenty-four hours. She needed to pack a few more things, grab a couple of essentials and clear her fridge. Then back here. To Tuscany. To Luciano.

Her gaze fell on the tall Italian. Luciano had been invited to the wedding and although he had skipped the dinner, had returned for the party. Not that it could be much of a party for him, trapped in a corner with several of Annabel's cousins and some of the other bridesmaids. She sent him a conspiratorial smile, her breath quickening when he returned it. His smile had always done funny things to her insides. Well, if she was going to stay around here then she would need to find some immunity. Maybe indigestion tablets would take care of that.

'What's going on between you two anyway?' Max asked, eyebrows high,

'Between you two who?' Liv prevaricated, cheeks instantly burning.

'You and Mr Tall, Dark and Italian over there? Moonlit walks, whispered conversations in corners, longing glances, secret smiles? Don't look so embarrassed, Liv, you deserve a bit of holiday fun, especially as this hasn't been much of a holiday for you. When I begged you to give Annabel a hand I meant with a bit of translation, not literally taking over all the last-minute details.'

Details that had kept her up to one in the morning and on the go from six this morning. She just hoped the fuchsia dress didn't bring out the shadows under her eyes. At least she had been too rushed to spend too much time bemoaning how little the style or colour suited her. If Liv was ever going to get married she would let the bridesmaids wear any damn colour they pleased. Scratch that, if Liv ever got married she was going to elope.

Not that marriage was on the cards right now considering her single status. A status she had never minded too much. After all, it was safer not to let anyone in; if she didn't care too much she couldn't get hurt. In the end, the few men who made it past the dating stage would get frustrated with her inability to open up, her need to guard her emotions, her heart, and she would end it, a self-fulfilling prophecy. Despite herself she stole another look at Luciano, and realised he was still looking over at her. Their eyes met and once again her chest tightened, her stomach swooping. Determinedly she dragged her gaze away and focused on her brother.

'As I said, happy to help and sorry to burst your romantic bubble but the only relationship I have with Luciano Del Visconti is a professional one.'

'Then don't waste any time dancing with your brother and go over there and unprofessionalise it. Otherwise you'll lose out to Bijou. She has apparently told all the other bridesmaids that tonight's the night.' It was Max's turn to look over at the corner where Luciano stood besieged. 'A fate worse than death. Go and rescue him, Liv.'

'He's a grown man, he can rescue himself,' she protested as Max steered them towards the corner and let her go, taking Bijou's hand and pulling her onto the dance floor.

'Dance with your new cousin by marriage, B,' he said, giving Liv an exaggerated wink. 'Luciano, do me a favour and dance with Liv seeing as I have abandoned her mid dance.'

'I am nobody's favour,' Liv said indignantly, her heartbeat accelerating as Luciano extended a hand towards her.

'No, but it would be an honour if you agreed.'

The bridesmaids behind him sighed and Liv couldn't repress an answering smile. 'Well, okay, thank you. But don't feel as if you have to just because my brother is an idiot.'

But she couldn't deny the thrill that ran through every nerve as Luciano took her hand in his and spun her onto the floor, nor a moment of petty victory as the small group of Annabel's friends and relatives who had been clustered around Luciano glared at her incredulously.

'This is going to do nothing to quell the rumours that we are having some kind of holiday fling,' she told Luciano severely. 'I should have made Max leave you in Bijou's tender clutches.'

She wanted to recall the words as soon as she had said them. Cattiness was not her style; maybe Luciano had been quite content in Bijou's clutches, maybe he had enjoyed being at the centre of an adoring, hair-flicking, lip-gloss-applying, eyelashes-batting group. And there she was, being catty again.

'Thank you for rescuing me, I was just

about to make up a wine emergency,' he said, face perfectly solemn but laughter dancing in his dark eyes.

'What kind of wine emergency?'

'A fermentation failure.'

'Is that even a real thing?'

'If it had got me out of that corner then yes, as real as I needed it to be.'

'Who knew you were so sly?' she marvelled.

Liv was aware of more than a few people watching them, some amused, some smiling indulgently, some clearly envious but she didn't feel self-conscious. The dance floor was set up at one end of the walled garden, softly lit by lanterns and strings of white fairy lights, tables and chairs encircling it. Beyond lay a buffet table groaning with plates of cheese and cured meats, olives and grapes, small cakes and fruit, although how anyone had any appetite after the lavish feast they had enjoyed earlier she had no idea. The air was filled with citrus, the stars bright in the sky above, the evening air warm on her bare arms.

'Your home is so beautiful,' she said dreamily.

'No regrets about staying?'

'None, I just need to bite the bullet and tell my family.'

'They'll be upset?'

'Concerned, exasperated. Worried. Losing my job, taking up unstable temporary work abroad, no master plan for what's next? Of course they'll be shocked. You know, I have done everything that was asked of me. Good school results, university even if it wasn't as prestigious as they would have liked or a degree they understood, a city firm. I own my flat, I have a healthy savings account. And yet they just don't take me seriously. My family will always see me as that dreamy teenager who would rather read than debate.' She sighed.

'Whereas I see a resourceful woman who is strong enough to reframe a disappointment as a challenge.' Luciano's gaze was warm. 'Maybe they will too. Maybe you are underestimating them. They clearly love you.'

'They love me and they worry about me. Every single one of my family has a master plan for life, my mother has hers in a spreadsheet. They are driven and ambitious and they want that drive and ambition for me too. I get it. My mother came from a horribly unstable background, she worked her arse off to get to

Cambridge, to become a barrister, a judge. She ensured we wanted for nothing, her and Dad, did her best to instil in us that same drive. But I just don't have it.'

'I don't think that's true. I think you do have it, but for different things. I used to see how your eyes lit up in a gallery, talking about the paintings you loved. How you came alive discovering Florence, making your home there. It's a shame you put that to one side to try and be the person your family think you should be rather than the person you are.'

Liv couldn't maintain eye contact, couldn't cope with how vulnerable he made her feel. She wasn't used to being seen like this. 'My parents had always said they would pay for a law conversion but not for any other post-grad qualification. I had planned to go it alone, to do an MA in art history anyway. But when I got back from Florence…' She stopped. How could she tell him that once he had left so suddenly all the magic had gone from the city, that her certainty in herself, in her path, had ebbed? It wouldn't be fair to put that on him. Besides, her feelings, her decisions, she needed to own them. 'It was generous of them,' she said instead. 'And the rest of my family seemed happy with their choices.

It's not easy always being the odd one out. I hoped that I would find that same happiness if I followed in their footsteps, but if I am honest I hated every minute. It was a relief when my firm let me go. It *is* a relief.'

The song ended and she stood back, aware that too many eyes were still on them. 'Go dance with Bijou,' she said.

'I'm sorry, I thought you were ordering me to go and dance with a woman named after a description.'

'It's not her fault that her parents were predictably unpredictable. And I'm not your employee yet. In fact I am the woman who did you a huge favour and therefore is probably owed a favour in return.

Luciano's eyes gleamed, his mouth tipping into the ghost of a smile with just enough wolf to make her stomach clench. 'And this is the favour you choose?' he asked softly.

'Luciano, you can't single me out like this. Bijou, Araminta, Tallulah or Great-Aunt Charity, I don't mind who you choose but choose someone.'

'Your wish is my command.' Luciano half bowed and backed away before turning and walking, not over to Bijou but to the corner where Liv's Great-Aunt Charity sat tapping her foot. A headmistress at a prestigious girl's school, she dressed in the kind of power suits that had been in and out of fashion so much since the eighties they had become timeless. Liv watched, unable to hide her smile as Luciano stopped in front of her great-aunt and extended a hand, just as he had for her earlier. A hand her great-aunt accepted with her usual dignity.

'He's quite the charmer.'

Liv jumped and turned around to find her mother by her side.

'He's a good host.' She looked around for something she could use to distract her mother from the dangerous topic of Luciano's charm. 'Don't Max and Annabel look gorgeous? It's been a beautiful wedding.'

'In no small part thanks to you,' her mother said tartly. 'I've hardly seen you all week. In fact, if I didn't know better, I would think you were avoiding me.'

Liv tried to look guileless as she snagged a glass of something cold and fizzy and alcoholic from a passing waiter with a thankful smile. 'Avoid you?' she said with an attempt at the overused neutral smile. 'Of course not. Why would I do that?'

Now why had she used an open question

and given her mother an in? Bad mistake, Liv. Amateur.

'I have been wondering the same thing. At first I wondered if you were missing Josh, but you made it clear *you* broke up with him.'

'I did, yes.'

'And then I got a message from Lionel.'

'Oh.' For the second time in a two-minute window Liv's stomach swooped, only this time in apprehension. 'How is he?'

'Hoping that I recognise his decision to terminate your contract was professional not personal and that it won't affect our friendship.'

'Ah.'

'What really upset me,' her mother continued, 'was that you didn't tell me yourself.'

'I was going to, Mum. But I didn't want to ruin the wedding. I had planned to tell you tomorrow.'

'I knew we needed a summit. It's going to be a rush now. You'll just have to come back home with us so your father and I have enough time to start looking at contacts. I assume there is an NDA on both sides and your settlement comes with excellent references. I'll get Portia to come back with us too. You'll need her advice.'

So, the showdown was going to be today

after all. ‘No, Mum, don’t disrupt Portia’s plans. I don’t need a summit.’

‘Portia mentioned efficiencies. How on earth were *you* caught up in those? What was the criteria?’

‘Billable hours and in my case a lack of them—and I’m glad, Mum. I want a lunch break and to leave on time. I want to take my holidays without an expectation that I am always available. I meant what I said the other day, I need a change. Maybe to travel, maybe something else, but I don’t want to waste my life totting up minutes spent reading clauses to earn money I am too tired to spend on anything that makes life meaningful.’ Liv searched her mother’s face for any clue her mother was hearing her, understood.

‘Maybe a non-profit would suit you better. Celeste might have some ideas.’

‘Maybe, at some point but not now. I actually have something lined up, you don’t need to worry.’

‘What? Already? Where? Olivia, there are plenty of opportunities in High Street firms now so if you are moving to one don’t be ashamed…’

‘Mum! It’s not a High Street firm…’

‘Thank goodness!’

'It's not law at all. I am coming back here to take care of the weddings and other events until the end of the season.' Liv tilted her chin and waited for her mother's reaction.

'Back here? But why? What do *you* know about weddings?'

'I've been to at least twenty in the last four years so I must know something.'

'That's hardly the same thing…'

'If the law trained me for anything it's being detail orientated and that's what Luciano needs along with someone fluent in Italian and English. I am available, I know the team and I am enjoying being here, doing something different, something varied. Besides, look at this place!'

'But…'

Liv slipped a hand through her mum's arm. 'Mum, I need some time. I haven't been happy for a long time now. In fact, I don't think work wise I have ever been happy. I'd come home and see you and Dad and Max and Portia talking about your cases and industry gossip and you were all so alive and animated and I… I just didn't know what to say. Wonder why for me it was some huge chore, why I couldn't feel the way you all did. Why I didn't fit in.'

'And you fit in here?'

'It's not a permanent solution.' Liv looked over at Luciano, who now was approaching Bijou, head high like a man walking towards his fate, and for a moment she allowed herself to remember how safe she had felt in his arms, the thrill of being the sole focus of his dark-eyed attention. 'But it's a step.'

She just hoped it was the right one and this wouldn't prove to be a monumental mistake.

'You came back.' Luciano opened the taxi door and helped Liv step out. He was surprised by how pleased he was to see her, how he had been anticipating the taxi, unable to settle down to anything until he saw it pull in. Of course he needed her professionally; it was the role not the woman he was relieved about.

At least, that was what he was going to keep telling himself until he believed it.

Liv raised her eyebrows. 'Coming back was the plan, why the surprise?'

'I thought you might change your mind.'

'Or my family might change it for me? They had a go, but their hearts weren't in it. I think they knew that I was set on this.' Liv stretched. 'Oof. I have no idea how people do extreme day trips, a twenty-four-hour turnaround was bad enough.'

The taxi driver deposited the suitcases beside them and accepted the tip Luciano handed him with a smile. Liv watched him drive off.

'That's it, I am abandoned to my fate in the castle,' she said. 'Bring me your stressed brides and detail-orientated mothers of the bride, your nervous grooms and uninformed ushers, I am ready.'

'Maybe we should settle you in first,' Luciano suggested.

'Is that a subtle way of saying "Take a shower, Liv"?'

She seemed freer, lighter. Like now that her parents knew about her job situation and she had made the decision to stay a burden had been lifted. He wished he felt so sure. Offering Liv the job had felt like a good idea at the time, but dancing with her at the wedding had brought back too many memories, the warmth of her body pressed against his, the scent of her, the way she touched him, assured and confident. It was hard to hold her and not be transported back to that night, to the moment he had known that this was it, that they were finally nearing the end of the dance they had been embarked on for months. There was unfinished business between Liv and him. Business he had no right to resurrect, especially as she would now be his employee. It was safer all round if he maintained a professional, respectful distance. No more stars, no more moonlit dances, no more intimate conversations, just work updates and polite chit-chat.

So he wasn't going to start her employment by commenting on her need or not for a shower, or thinking about her in a shower, wondering how those new subtle curves looked highlighted by the water, her hair wet and slicked back, no, definitely not the latter. He signalled for one of the waiting men to take her cases and set off, Liv by his side.

'I think Portia was desperate to offer sisterly advice,' Liv continued. 'But Mum has been amazing, it's like she recognises I need time. I'm sure she'll snap out of it soon and the family chat will be full of helpful tips and contacts but for now I am going to enjoy the peace. Oh, where are we going?'

Luciano had led her into the grand wide hallway which was the very centre of the Castello. 'The room you had before is a guest room, so we have moved you to the main house. Francesca packed up your things. I hope that's okay.'

'I wouldn't have left things in such a mess if I'd realised, I'll have to grovel to her.'

The room Luciano had allotted Liv was in the main Castello, in the family apartment which occupied the first and second floors. It was a sensible decision, as the apartment was huge with six ensuite bedrooms on two floors, several sitting rooms and studies. The kitchen, dining rooms and formal reception rooms as well as the library were on the ground floor, although there was a small kitchenette in the apartment for late-night snacks and quick breakfasts. With Elisabetta away there was plenty of room for someone else, several someone elses, but he hadn't considered what it would be like with just the two of them sharing the space. Even a space as large as the medieval keep.

'This is beautiful, how thick are these stone walls? Is it all original? Are these portraits all your ancestors?'

Liv kept up a steady stream of questions as he took her to her room and Luciano was grateful; answering gave him little time for second-guessing. Her room was at the opposite end of the keep to his, a large square room with tall shuttered windows and double doors leading out onto a small terrace furnished with a table and chairs overlooking the gardens and vineyards beyond.

The room was painted a restful sage green, vine-patterned curtains at the windows, matching cushions on the king-sized bed and on the chair and chaise, which created a cosy sitting corner. The furniture was all antique, but carefully preserved, the wood polished to a warm honey, the floorboards covered by rugs.

'This is you, I hope you'll be comfortable,' he said as he opened the door and ushered her in. 'The bathroom is through there, it should be stocked but if there is anything you need just let Francesca know. There is a small sitting room next door you can use and you'll find a small kitchenette further down the corridor for drinks and snacks.'

Liv turned around, her grey eyes wide. 'I was expecting servants' quarters in the attic, not a room fit for a duchess. I think I'll manage.'

'Great. As you know there's always breakfast, lunch and dinner available over in the office wing for those working. But if you prefer to eat at a different time or want something different the main family kitchen is downstairs, we usually cater for ourselves there.'

'What, no formal dinner at nine every night

waited on by solemn footmen with matching heights, chosen for their leg muscles? I'll need to readjust my expectations but I think I can manage. Give me an hour to unpack and change and I'll get to it. I'm in Elisabetta's office still, I suppose?'

'Yes, can you find your way there?'

'If I'm not there in two hours send out the hounds. Have the next party arrived yet?'

Luciano shook his head. 'It's a shorter booking. They don't come until Wednesday, so you have a couple of days to settle in. We do need to discuss hours and days off. I am aware that last week wasn't much of a holiday for you.'

Liv grinned. 'I was quite happy having an excuse to duck out of all the organised fun but I would like to explore if I get a chance. I've been promising myself a return trip to Florence ever since I left and now I've got a taste for extreme day trips I might venture further afield.'

'We have a small island near Capri you are welcome to use, but you would need to spend several days there.'

'Part of those mystery family estates? That sounds incredible. I *was* thinking more of the fast train to Rome…'

'Roma in the *summer*?'

She laughed. 'Spoken like a true Italian, but I am a mere tourist. I dug some of my old notes and a couple of books out last night, thought I might make a note of any museums or galleries I want to visit and base an itinerary around them. But I am also aware I am being wildly optimistic. If last week is a guide all I'll be fit for on any time off is flopping by the pool.'

'Hopefully we won't work you as hard as that. Like I say, week-long bookings are rare, five days is more manageable. Okay,' he said as he backed towards the door. 'I'll leave you to settle in.'

'Thank you.' She turned to look at him. 'I mean, seriously, thank you. For the job, for this beautiful room, for dancing with Great-Aunt Charity…'

'Now that was a pleasure, I liked her very much. As for the room, it's the least I could do. We need you more than you need us, remember?'

'I wonder.'

Their eyes met, held, the moment stretching, palpable. It took every bit of self-control to stay standing by the door, to not stride over to her, to pull her close. Her eyes were wide, lips parted, she seemed as under the spell as he and he knew, deep and primal, that if he made a move she wouldn't stop him.

No, knowing Liv she would meet him halfway. He couldn't remember who had kissed who eight years ago, only that the knowledge it was time was building in the air all evening, every word, every glance, every touch leading them there.

But that was then. He stepped back, broke the spell and with one last. tight smile left the room.

Luciano had intended to head straight to his office, but instead he found himself climbing the stairs to the top floor. He now had a suite of rooms on the second floor, but as a boy had slept up here. He didn't head to his boyhood bedroom, with its single bed and football posters on the wall, incongruous next to the prints of famous paintings interspersed among them, but to the room next door, a corner room, windows on two sides flooding the space with light. This room and all within it had been a present from Meg, when Elisabetta was born. A space of his own.

He stood outside for a moment, deliberately slowing his breathing, his hand on the door handle. Slowly he opened the door. He hadn't been in this room since the accident, but someone had. It was clean, the wooden floor swept clear of dust, the cubbyholes and shelves tidy, brushes and pens and paper stacked neatly, the sink clean, brushes in a pot on the draining board as if he had stepped out of here just a day ago.

An easel stood near the window, an A3 piece of paper still pinned to it. Luciano stepped over to it, touched the paper, inhaling the scent of wood and paper. Something was missing, the sharp tang of paint.

He had always preferred watercolours for abstracts or landscapes, layering colour and shade, creating the ideas of shape and place rather than faithful recreations. Portraits were usually pencil, or pen and ink. Pinned to the wall was the last one he had done of Meg, her hair escaping as usual from a messy bun, her eyes laughing. He'd been planning to get it framed for her birthday.

The paints were dry, unusable, but the pencils were lined up inviting him, some sharp, some blunt, tools lack of use had not allowed him to forget how to employ. Almost in a daze he stepped over to the easel and removed the piece of paper, pinning a fresh sheet in its place, and without thought, selected a pencil, and began to draw, grey eyes, a pointed chin and a wistful smile clear in his mind.

# CHAPTER SIX

'IT'S FUNNY,' LIV SAID, stretching. 'A week in that law office felt like eternity, but I have been here a month and it feels like two minutes.'

'That's because you haven't stopped,' Luciano pointed out as he took the seat opposite her, his usual espresso in hand. Liv looked at the thick dark liquid and shuddered; she knew Luciano considered her milky coffee fit only for children. She cradled her mug protectively.

'I didn't then, what with every second billable,' she said. 'But this feels different. Every *task* is different. It changes how the day goes, changes time. Work doesn't feel interminable the way it did, the way I accepted it did.'

'You're not regretting staying then?'

'Regretting? Oh no. I've not slept so well in years, nor eaten so well.' She picked up a slice of a fresh nectarine from the platter of fruit in the centre of the breakfast table to illustrate her point. 'The only thing is I have been far too busy to think about what comes next, which is either a blessing or a curse, I haven't figured out which one yet.'

'Do you have to figure it out now?'

'Not this second, no, I am embracing the whole spontaneous thing, but I also don't want to get to October with still no idea about what comes next. The friend of Max's who's staying in my flat this summer is interested in renting it longer term but obviously wants a year-long contract. It means the mortgage is taken care of for the foreseeable so I am inclined to say yes, but it means I will need to think about somewhere to live as well as something to do.'

'You can stay here as long as you need. I promise we won't kick you out the second the last bride says "I do".'

'The last groom—the last wedding is two grooms—but that's reassuring. But careful what you promise, otherwise in fifty years' time your grandchildren will ask who the strange lady at the end of the corridor is.'

Liv took another slice of the nectarine. She took most of her meals in the staff dining room, the food fresh, tasty and plentiful, but she'd started early that morning and missed breakfast, so had decided to stop and have some coffee and a light snack outside and enjoy the sun. Only she hadn't expected to see Luciano there. Clearly he had had the same idea. This was the first time she had sat tête-à-tête with Luciano since she had returned from London four weeks ago. In fact, she had hardly seen him at all. It wasn't that she had been avoiding him exactly, and she didn't think *he* was avoiding *her* exactly, but there seemed to be a tacit understanding that there would be no more dances or evening walks. That their old relationship was to be forgotten, the new one they were forging strictly professional.

She took a sip of coffee and watched Luciano through her sunglasses. Something was different. He seemed freer somehow, lighter. He still started work early but left the office before dinner and didn't return. Maybe he was dating. That would be great for him, absolutely none of her business and that was not a stab of possessive jealousy at the thought.

Grabbing her phone, Liv opened her email, needing to distract herself from a series of increasingly vivid mental images of Luciano and a beautiful mystery woman dancing, kissing, gazing at each other. Her mother was right; her overactive imagination was a curse. She read an email, realised she hadn't taken in a word, then read it again. It still didn't make sense.

'Liv?' She looked up to see Luciano regarding her with a mixture of amusement and slight exasperation.

'I'm sorry, I was…' *Fantasising about you and your mystery woman who might be as imaginary as my childhood dog.* 'Miles away.'

'I noticed.'

'I'm all attention now.'

'I said isn't today your day off?'

'Yes,' she admitted.

'But you've been in the office since seven?'

He'd noticed. 'I haven't really got any plans and there is so much to do…'

'What about your list of galleries?'

So much for her grand plans. 'Slight issue in that I haven't managed to compile it yet. It's just been so full on. I have time still.'

Luciano pushed his chair back. 'Right, that's it. I'm stepping in. I'll meet you out front in fifteen minutes. We are going to Florence.'

Liv sat, aware her mouth was open and she was gaping at Luciano as if he had suggested that they were going to Mars. 'But…'

'But what?'

'Surely you have better things to do than drive me to Florence. It's nice of you but honestly, I am fine. Point taken. I'll take some time off. Today.'

'Fifteen minutes,' he said aggravatingly as if she hadn't said anything. 'Don't keep me waiting.'

'I...' But he had gone. 'Of all the high-handed, bossy men! Don't be late indeed.' But she was on her feet and heading to the stair quickly calculating what she needed. Her linen midi skirt and teal silk top would do. She just needed a bit of make-up, her bag, a light jacket for later. Because of course she was going. Not because Luciano had made it clear she couldn't refuse but because she wanted to return to the city which had won her heart eight years ago.

And she wanted to go with the man who had broken her heart there, even though she knew it was probably a Bad Idea.

It took considerably less time than the fifteen minutes allotted for Liv to get ready but she didn't head back straight downstairs, carefully timing herself so she reached the driveway exactly fifteen minutes after Luciano had issued his command. She was hoping he would be late but he was waiting for her, leaning against a red convertible sports car she hadn't seen before.

'Utter cliché,' she muttered, but she wasn't even fooling herself. There was something inherently sexy about a confident man in a beautiful car, and when the man was as gorgeous as Luciano the sexiness was ramped up to almost unbearable levels. Liv took in a long, deep inhale and walked over.

'Not a bad little motor,' she said nonchalantly.

'Here.' Luciano handed her a scarf. 'For your hair.'

Liv took the folded silk square. 'How well prepared.'

'Elisabetta always forgets to tie her hair up and insists on having the top down no matter the weather. I've learned to have a supply with me.'

So the scarf was Elisabetta's not the imaginary mystery woman's. Liv tied it around her hair and got into the car, feeling like a fifties film star. If only she'd worn a glamorous fifties-style dress and not a sensible skirt.

It was difficult to make conversation once they set off. Without a roof the sounds of the road and countryside were amplified and so, after a few tries at chatting, Liv settled back in her seat and enjoyed the ride. Luciano was a consummate driver, the car purring around bends, his hands relaxed on the wheel. Liv tried to concentrate on the scenery and the road ahead but she found herself sneaking peeks at her companion, noting the strong, capable hands, the cords in his wrists, the breadth of his shoulders. The vee at his throat. His aquiline nose, the curve of his jaw, the outline of his mouth. Taken individually each of these features was attractive. Together they were devastating. Liv was all too aware of his every shift and glance, her own body lighting up like Christmas decorations with every occasional glance or smile.

She couldn't deny it; the crush she had had eight years ago had resurfaced stronger than ever even though she knew exactly how this situation ended. She just needed to remember all the reasons why giving into her feelings was a bad idea. It was just much easier to do that when she wasn't crammed into a tiny car with Luciano within touching distance. She folded her hands into her lap, trying not to wish it was his hand in hers.

This was why she should be keeping her distance. But she couldn't deny how much she was enjoying the sweet torture of their intimate proximity.

All too soon the familiar sight of the Florence skyline came into view and the fizzing in Liv's stomach increased.

'*La bella*,' she murmured, remembering her first sight of the city, how instantly and hard she had fallen, how she had revelled in being a local not a tourist. She looked around eagerly as Luciano drove in, seeking out every familiar landmark, every subtle change.

Luciano drove to a small private garage and parked up. Liv was glad of the courteous hand he gave her to help her out the car, the low seats and cramped leg space ensuring an impossible dignified exit.

'Okay,' Luciano said. 'I have some business to take care of and then I'll probably get something to eat. Let's meet back here at six, or if you want to stay out later and get a taxi back just drop me a text.'

So they *weren't* spending the day together. Liv tried to shake off her disappointment. Hadn't she just been telling herself that distance was better? It was certainly safer than a day of reminiscing in the city filled with the ghosts of their pasts.

'Great,' she said brightly. 'Let me just note down where we are and I'll see you back here. Thanks for the lift.'

For a moment she thought he was going to

say something more but instead he inclined his head and turned away. Liv stood paralysed for a second before turning herself, walking away as if this had been her plan all along, head high and body relaxed.

The street Liv exited on was unfamiliar but she knew this city of old, its landmarks and ebbs and flows, and it wasn't long before she was in familiar territory. The tall buildings, some golden stone, some painted reds and creams, welcomed her like an old friend. It was as if she had returned home and her step lightened the further she walked as she drank in the city and the people. Her first stop was a tiny ristorante where she ordered a coffee, drinking it standing up at the bar like a local, reaccustoming her ears to the Florentine dialect, to the rhythm of the city.

Florence was busier than she remembered, hotter, but of course eight years ago she had left before the height of summer. It was a relief to slip inside one of her favourite haunts, the Santa Maria Novella, and find some shade. Liv had always found peace in this beautiful old church, in the arched ceilings, tall pillars and marble floors, the scent of incense, the light filtered through the ornate stained glass windows. She made her way to the Great Cloister, where she had spent many hours studying the frescos. They were as vivid as she remembered, the frescos as breathtaking as ever, but she didn't lose herself in them the way she had when she was younger. Appreciated, yes, absolutely but not absorbed. It was impossible to switch off entirely, details about the forthcoming weddings darting into her mind, unanswered emails gnawing at her conscience. And through it all unwanted thoughts of Luciano, wondering what he was doing, if he was thinking of her.

Ugh. She was a more hopeless case than she had been back then.

After she left the church Liv contemplated her next steps, deciding to bypass the more famous galleries; she hadn't bought tickets in advance and had no desire to join the queues snaking down the street ready to tick another place off their bucket list. Instead she continued to visit old haunts, lesser-known museums, churches, galleries on hidden back streets, searching for that same sense of purpose that had filled her while she lived here. But although she gloried in rediscovering the city which had so completely captured her heart, she found herself more interested in people watching, in the architecture, in the old squares and ornate bridges as she strolled along the Arno than in losing herself in paintings and statues, much as she enjoyed them.

So that was one thing decided. She wouldn't be returning to study and attempting to turn the clock back and restart a career in art history. She still loved discovering the paintings but they no longer called to her. Out of practice or just a different person? Liv wasn't sure which.

She had intended to drop in at a church near where she used to live but instead she continued past, almost unconsciously walking the paths she had trodden every morning until she found herself at the gated courtyard entrance to her old home. The buildings surrounding the shaded courtyard were all made up of simple small studios let to students, to post grads, to creatives on a short-term basis. Liv had found her studio through the university and had thrilled at the idea of living so centrally. Her room had been tiny, a little kitchenette, a shower room barely big enough to hold the essentials, a high-ceilinged room which held a bed, a chest of drawers, a desk and chair. But she had been happy here, maybe the happiest she had ever been. Until this summer. She was busy, yes, with long days and a million demands on her time. She certainly hadn't found the elusive work-life balance she had felt in such desperate need of, but she was really enjoying the work. She liked the people and the problem solving and the variety, liked that she was on her feet as much as she was at a desk. Loved the location, the Castello starting to feel like home.

But it wasn't home. Not hers anyway. Nor was the job. She was just place holding.

Liv stepped back, allowing herself one last, lingering look at the courtyard and turned only to walk straight into something hard. Into someone. She looked up, words of apology on her lips, only to stop as she realised she had collided with Luciano.

'What are you doing here?'

She regretted the words as soon as she spoke them. He had as much right as she to be here—for that matter what was *she* doing, mooning around old haunts nostalgically? Liv tried to ignore the jolt of delight and anticipation shooting through her as she took him in. She felt crumpled and hot from walking around the city. Luciano on the other hand looked as cool and tempting as a large glass of iced water in his still perfectly pressed trousers and the short-sleeved shirt which showed off every sinew in the arms she had been admiring earlier. Even the tote bag he was carrying looked fresh and stylish.

Hang on, he hadn't had that earlier. Her gaze snagged on the logo and she mentally translated the words. 'You've bought art supplies!'

*'Si.'* For a moment he looked boyishly uncertain, the change from his usual confident self devastatingly adorable. 'I've started painting again, not like before, just a little dabbling.'

'So that's where you have been going every night?' Damn it, that was Advantage Luciano. 'Not that I have been noticing or wondering. I mean it's your business.'

Shut. Up. Liv.

But for all her embarrassment she was also aware of something that felt like relief. Luciano wasn't dating someone; it wasn't a relationship that accounted for his abstraction or absence or lift in mood. Not that it should matter to her.

But it did. Of course it did. There was a reason they had tacitly agreed to spend less time together. That old attraction had never gone away, it was still there, the undercurrent to every word, every interaction. And where better to acknowledge that than here, right where they had first met? Where their relationship had played out until the sudden end.

'Do you want to go in?' Luciano gestured to the gate.

'No keys, remember?'

'Sure about that?' He dug in his pocket and pulled out a small key.

'How do you still have that? They might have changed the locks, it's been eight years.' The gate swung open and Luciano gestured for her to go first. 'Or maybe not.' Liv took a tentative step forward and walked through the gate.

It was like going back in time. The courtyard was just as she remembered it, the same floral and herb-filled scent in the air, the same wrought iron tables and chairs in shady corners and arbours, the same sense of peace even within the heart of the city. Her steps took her unerringly to the door on the right of the courtyard. It was open and within she could see the hallway with doors on either side, the winding staircase leading up to the first and second floors.

'This was me,' she said, her voice a little hoarse. 'You were upstairs.'

Luciano didn't answer but started up the

stairs and after a moment she followed him. Her room had been on the ground floor and his two levels above, in the attic with sloping ceilings and access to a small roof terrace. Liv reached the top just as Luciano opened the door.

'You still rent the apartment?' she asked, surprised. Luciano had walked away from his past so comprehensively, why would he still keep a small studio in Florence?

'My family own these apartments. I own them,' he corrected.

'You were my *landlord*?'

'My father was back then.'

'Part of those mysterious estates you manage?'

'Something like that.'

Islands off Capri, real estate in the heart of Florence as well as the Castello and the vineyards, and Liv got the sense they were just the tip of the iceberg. How rich was Luciano exactly? Not that it mattered to her. She looked around the room, taking it in.

'It looks exactly the same but different.'

He laughed. 'Cleaner? Less cluttered?'

'Something like that.' The studio had always been big, twice the size of hers, but had felt smaller thanks to the easel by the window, the paper and paints and canvases stacked on tables and against walls. Luciano had cheerfully admitted that he wasn't the tidiest of artists, flitting between projects and mediums and subjects. Now the room was tidy, clean, stark. Just the kitchenette on one side, a sofa and coffee table before them and the bed in the far corner.

'I think I preferred it before,' she said. 'The clutter was part of you.'

'I was trying to find myself then. Figure out what kind of artist I wanted to be, whether I was merely talented or something more.'

'I think we were all here trying to find ourselves.' Liv thought about her neighbours back then, fellow foreign students drawn to Florence by its name and beauty, dancers and singers and musicians, postgrads on the start of their academic careers, other artists, writers. A space full of youth and untried ambition.

'What were you looking for, Liv?'

'Me?' He was standing close, looking down at her, his expression searching, intense, as if he wanted to see inside her soul. She shivered. 'I don't know.'

He didn't speak and the silence stretched as she asked herself the same question. 'I don't know,' she repeated. 'Maybe hope that I was different, could be different, that I could divert from the path laid out for me?'

'Is that what you are doing now? Diverting?' His voice was low, a rasp that licked against every nerve.

'The thing about being twenty-one is you think you have it sussed, that the world is there for the taking. That you are different, special, bolder. And then another year passes and the safety net of university falls away and you realise you aren't so special any more and maybe the safest option isn't the cop-out you used to believe. But I am older now and finally ready to spread my wings. Ready to leap.'

Was Liv talking about herself, about him or about them? Luciano no longer knew.

'What about you? Why haven't you let this room? Why keep it?' she asked.

'I'm not sure,' he admitted. 'It's not as if I will ever use it again. It had occupants before me, there's nothing particularly special about it. I suppose in a way…' He stopped.

'In a way what?'

'I feel like I left some of my soul here,' he admitted, immediately wishing he could take the words back. Turning the clock back had never been an option and he and Elisabetta had lost a lot more than his freedom to paint, to choose his own path that June night. But Liv didn't look appalled or worse, pitying; instead her expression was full of understanding and compassion.

'Do you come here often?'

'Hardly ever. Not for several years. Looking back wasn't something I could afford to do before.'

'Before what?' But he could see that she already knew the answer.

'Before you. Seeing you again, Liv, it's impossible not to look back. Not to remember the boy I was.'

Dangerous words, highlighting the charge between them. Words once said that couldn't be recalled. But he didn't want to recall them. He was aware that her gaze kept flicking to the bed in the corner, that her pupils were dilated and her breath quick and shallow. He was aware of the blood roaring around his body, in his veins, the pound of his heart pulsing at every point.

He was aware that he had known he would find her here in these old haunts, that he had come here to seek her out, that away from the Castello and their roles there everything felt different.

He was aware that the sensible thing to do would be to step away, defuse the electricity prickling through the atmosphere, make his excuses and leave. But he was tired of being sensible. He couldn't just leave. Wouldn't.

In the shuttered light Liv looked just as she had eight years ago, her hair loose, floating around her shoulders, her eyes luminous. She had always been pretty but her prettiness was the kind that was lit from within, through a smile or an expression or a flash from her grey eyes; it made her maddeningly elusive to paint. And he had tried. Then and now.

'Is that why you are painting again?' she half whispered. 'Because you are looking back?'

'I'm painting again because there is something I want to paint.' Slowly, deliberately he put the bag down on the empty coffee table before reaching out and tracing the line of her face. Her skin was silk under his fingertip and she quivered under his touch. 'I locked it all away. Painting, the memory of what we shared, everything that wasn't surviving.'

Her eyes were wide, fixed on his face. 'Is it so bad, remembering?'

'Depends on the memory.' He ran his finger along the curve of her full lips. 'Turns out some of the memories should never have been locked away.'

Touching her, reliving the past, they were everything he had promised himself not to do, but equally they had felt inevitable from the moment she had walked into his study. Luciano had done his best to keep his distance over the last few weeks but she was everywhere he looked, her laugh, her voice always audible around the next corner, glimpses of her bright hair in the office, in the grounds, in his home. In his head. On the many pieces of paper on which he failed to capture just what made her *her.* Seeing her outside the courtyard had felt inevitable. Fate drawing them together for a reason.

And what man could fight fate?

'No,' she said, still looking up at him, her heart and soul in her eyes. 'Our memories are there for a reason. To comfort, to amuse, to warn.'

*To warn.* Those words weren't chosen at random.

'I hurt you last time.' It was a statement.

'You did. I understand why, but for a long time I didn't. How could I? I won't let you hurt me again.'

Luciano couldn't reply. He wouldn't make

promises he couldn't keep and how could he promise never to hurt her again? After all he hadn't meant to last time. Human hearts were fragile things, emotions wild and out of control. A man could do damage when he only intended good things. His hand was still resting against her cheek and he slowly dropped it to his side. 'I'm sorry.'

'No, don't apologise. What I mean is, I won't *let* you hurt me. I am older and hopefully wiser and I no longer have a head filled with romantic daydreams. This is a level playing field. Apart from the small fact that you are my boss. Temporarily anyway.'

'Apart from that.' Luciano tried to keep the smile from his face, she looked so determined, so serious.

She tilted her chin. 'If we do this, and I think that's where we are heading, then we need to establish some rules.'

'Are you sure you are not cut out to be a lawyer because this is all sounding very like a contract to me?'

'Contract, rules, the same thing. First, no promises we can't keep. Your life is here, mine is somewhere yet to be determined, but we have different futures, different responsibilities.'

'Agreed.'

'Secondly, our private life is just that, private. I don't want anyone back at the Castello to suspect we are anything but colleagues.'

'Also agreed.'

'Third, this is fun, nothing serious. We don't confuse attraction and chemistry with anything more serious. Fourth…' She screwed her nose up in thought. 'Maybe that's it. Private, temporary, no regrets.'

'Where do I sign? Actually,' he said and smiled down into her eyes, 'there is just one more thing to make the contract watertight. Can you define what *this* is?'

Liv stared up at him, contemplative, and then she smiled, slow, sweet, devilish. 'I can do better, I can show you.'

Now it was Luciano's turn to stand still as Liv reached up and drew a maddeningly slow finger down his face, down his jawline, tracing his lips, the touch burning a trail wherever she went, his body lighting up in response.

'No,' he managed, fighting the urge to pull her close. 'Still not getting it.'

She bit her lip, adorably confused for a moment before closing the space between them and pressing a feather-light kiss to his cheek, his jaw, a whisper of a kiss on his mouth, her hands the lightest of touches on his shoulders. Luciano endured the torture for a few more seconds and then gave into the increasingly loud demands of his body and pulled her in tight, his mouth finding hers, hard and insistent and needing. It was as if their last kiss had been yesterday not years before. He knew her, knew her taste, the way she felt, the way she gasped, the way she responded.

She was pressed close to him, the length of her leg against his, the swell of her breasts against his chest, her arms wrapped around his neck, her fingers tangled in his hair. Every single nerve and sinew was achingly aware of her proximity, the scent of her, the feel of her, the taste of her consuming him. Slowly but surely he backed her towards the bed, step by step, discarding clothes as they went, breaking the kiss long enough to remove her top. Luciano sucked in a breath as her breasts were revealed, barely covered by the small cream lace cups of her pretty bra. In return she worked feverishly at his shirt, pushing it off his shoulders triumphantly as he shucked it off. Then her skirt, crumpled on the floor as they reached the bed and he picked her up and deposited her on it. She lay propped on her elbows and looked up at him, eyes half shut, hair tangled around her shoulders, lips parted. Her pants matched her bra, a scrap of silk and lace, her body tanned and lean. Luciano held her gaze as he undid his belt, and within seconds his shoes and trousers joined her clothes and he was sitting next to her, his gaze tracing every inch of her body.

'So beautiful,' he said hoarsely, before leaning in to kiss her, slowly this time, taking his time, his weight on one arm while his free hand started to explore her, her breasts, the lace just covering her rosy nipples, the curve of her belly and hip, down to her thighs before coming to rest on the silk covering the centre of her, drawing tantalising slow circles on her skin, rediscovering what made her breath deepen and hitch.

Dropping a line of kisses down her throat and along her collarbone, Luciano unclipped her bra, sliding the straps down her shoulders to reveal her small perfect breasts, taking a moment to savour them before continuing the line of kisses down her body until he found first one nipple and then the other, finally slipping his hand inside the remaining scrap of silk as he did so. Liv moaned, her body shifting against him, pressing against his hand, urging him on. Luciano wanted to take his time, to savour every kiss, but Liv had other ideas, pulling him down, and pushing at his boxer shorts as she wiggled out of her own pants.

'Wait,' he half panted. 'Liv, are you sure?'

'Completely,' she said. 'We have a contract, remember?'

'Oh, I remember.' He pulled away reluctantly, leaning back over to kiss her long and deep, before groping for his trousers and the wallet in the back pocket, finding the small foil packet he kept there. Palming it he lay down beside her, sliding a leg over her, shifting into place. 'And I always fulfil my obligations to my fullest extent.'

'I'm counting on it,' Liv said as she took the packet from him. 'And I have very high standards.'

Then he was kissing her again and all thoughts, all words disappeared. There was only touch and sighs and moans, kisses and caresses and sensation until Luciano didn't know where he started and she ended. All he knew was that if they had just a short time together then he was going to make the most of every second.

# CHAPTER SEVEN

LIV FELT LIKE she was leading two lives and it was *delicious.* On one hand she was the events manager at a prestigious wedding venue, up early, late to bed, every moment in between filled with myriad tasks from customer service to sourcing any one of a million weird and wonderful things forthcoming brides and grooms felt essential for their perfect day, to table dressing and everything in between. The days of sitting at a desk staring at a screen until her eyes were dry and her head pounded felt a long time ago. She loved the variety of her days, the people she met, every wedding beautiful and unique and ever so slightly bonkers in its own way. She'd already booked several new weddings for the few vacant weeks in the following year and half the year after had now been confirmed, with some wine tasting and walking tours organised for the early autumn and spring.

There was a real sense of satisfaction in the work, but Liv had to keep reminding herself that she was merely placeholding and that she still had no idea what came next, despite her mother's many messages and the helpful job adverts sent through by her sister and Celeste. All she knew was that she *wasn't* going back to law and that her dreams of heading back into art history were just that, dreams. Academia for her was a hobby not a vocation.

The problem was she was finding it impossible to think about the future; she was too happy in the here and now, both in her work and in the other half of her life. The secret half. The half where she and Luciano snuck away to dark corners and behind closed doors. Liv shivered. She felt like a teenager again. Stolen kisses, sneaking down the corridor even though no one lived in the apartment but them. The very illicitness of the…fling, affair, arrangement?…was a thrill. Acting professionally in the office when all the time she knew exactly what he had been doing to her that morning, knew the look in his eyes and the sounds he made when she touched him was a trip she couldn't get enough of. They hadn't been back from Florence for twenty-four hours when their decision not to have sex in the Castello was overturned, the force field between them too strong.

Luciano had been the *what if* who had haunted all her past, brief relationships. Now he was the present and it was glorious.

Short-term but glorious.

Wrenching her mind back to her work, Liv read the email that had just popped into her inbox then sat back with a cry of dismay before grabbing her phone and dialling. It went straight to voicemail.

'Hi Hatty, Liv here from the Castello Del Visconti. I just wanted to say I received your message and not to worry. I'll take care of everything here. I am so sorry. Don't worry about calling me back, I'll put everything in an email. As you say you have insurance so we should be able to get things sorted pretty easily. Take care of yourself. Bye.'

She hung up and reread the email and then got to her feet and headed out of her office and into the main office to find Francesca. Luciano was in there, talking to one of the wine-marketing people and it was all she could do to act natural, to give them both the same casual smile, to say 'hi' naturally, her hand itching to reach out and touch him, to claim him. Instead, she sat on the corner of Francesca's desk and held out her phone, the email she'd received on the screen.

'Francesca, I just had an email from Harriet Myles, who is supposed to be coming on Wednesday, the Myles-Hatton wedding?'

*'Si?'*

'Only they are not coming. Apparently Hatty caught her fiancé kissing her sister at a family party yesterday and the wedding is off.'

Liv could feel the office come to a stop, every head turning towards her, the human drama capturing everyone. Poor Hatty, she had been so excited and bubbly in her calls and emails, easy-going and amenable, just excited for the wedding and the life they were planning to build afterwards. Plans she would not have the chance to do. Still, better to know now than go through with the wedding and find out later.

'The wedding is off?' Francesca repeated.

'Yes. I've left a message to say we will take care of everything. Obviously, she has paid in full and there is no cancellation refund this late but luckily she has insurance so you and I need to go through and itemise everything with receipts so I can send the costs through to her. First though we need to cancel what we can food-wise. The rooms are being turned over today but that's fine, it means they just need a light going over next Monday. The only real issue is what we do if any guest still turns up. Technically I suppose the rooms are paid for? It seems unlikely but you never know.'

She and Francesca went into emergency mode and by the afternoon anything that could be cancelled was. They supplied all the wine from the vineyard, had a barn full of chairs and covers and lights and props, and so usually they just brought in food, flowers and entertainment from outside along with any more unusual requests. Liv compiled a list as she went, making sure Hattie had everything she needed for the insurance. It was quicker to unravel a wedding than to put it together, especially with the ex-bride clearly in peak organisational mode. Liv suspected it was easier for Hattie to deal with the practical than the emotional side of her new reality.

'How are you doing?' She jumped at the interruption, looking up to see Luciano leaning on the open office door.

'Good. It's been a crazy morning but at least we have managed to cancel the meat and fish, and most of the produce. Too late for the fruit though, but I am sure we will manage to consume that between us. Poor Hattie. I hope the insurers pay out, her parents were very generous and the whole thing was going to be pretty lavish. Her sister! Imagine! I bet it's frosty at home right now.'

'Better to discover before than after.' He echoed her earlier thought.

'Oh, absolutely. Can you imagine if she found them kissing at the wedding? Not the kind of testimonial we want. "The pool was beautiful and deep enough for me to push my traitorous sister and cheating new husband into."'

'Do you have much else you need to do?'

'Me? No. I think I have done everything I can right now for this. The next happy couple aren't due until a week on Wednesday.' She blinked as the reality of what the cancellation meant for her sunk in. 'That gives me time to catch up with the paperwork, I suppose.'

'Or you could take some time off? Take advantage of the unexpected free time.'

'I guess.' What was wrong with her? Luciano was right. She could head off for a few days, see some of the art galleries on the list she had failed to compile. Head to Rome or Venice or Verona. See famous monuments, buy tickets for the ballet or the opera, eat delicious food. She *wanted* to do all that. But she didn't want to miss out on a single secret moment with Luciano.

Ugh, she was pathetic. This fling or affair or whatever it was, was supposed to be under control. A way of working him out of her system, not embedding him even further in.

'You're right.' She tried to sound more enthusiastic. 'I should see what's possible at short notice, it could be fun to have a mini-break.'

'I was thinking about taking a short trip to the island. I haven't been this year.'

'I cannot believe you own an island. If I had one I would be there every weekend.' She put on a posh voice. *'Just heading off to my island. Oh, nothing special, just a luxury villa and my own private beach.'*

'I was thinking,' he continued, a half smile tilting his mouth, 'of going there today and I was also thinking of inviting you to come with me.'

Her heart sped up. 'Inviting me to the island? Just you and me?'

'There are a couple of live-in members of staff but otherwise yes, just you and me. If that sounds acceptable?'

It sounded a *lot* more than acceptable. Liv's mouth was dry as she stared across the office at him. 'But what about the privacy clause in our verbal contract?' His eyes gleamed and her stomach tightened; she knew he loved it when she talked legalese to him. 'Won't people talk if we disappear off just the two of us?'

He shrugged, gracefully careless. 'Let them.'

'What is there to do on this island?'

'Swim, sail, explore the beautiful Amalfi Coast and Capri.' He paused. 'Whatever else you can think of.'

'I might have a few ideas.' She allowed her gaze to sweep closely over him and he gave her a wolfish smile that undid her.

'I thought you might. Can you be ready to leave in an hour?'

'I'll see what I can do.'

Within the hour Liv was packed and waiting, anticipation thudding through her, both at the thought of the location—a private island would get the family group chat sitting up and taking notice!—and at the prospect of several days alone with Luciano. Maybe it was foolish to agree to spend dedicated time with him in this way, as it was almost definitely breaking the terms of the verbal contract she had half-jokingly, half-seriously proposed, but Liv didn't care. From the moment she had decided to stay, no, before that, from the moment she had signed the NDA when negotiating her payout from her old firm, she had felt free for the first time in a long time. Free and ready to live for today, not for a tick list of achievements. And this kind of impulsiveness was exactly what she needed.

Liv was expecting Luciano to be driving the sporty red convertible and had packed lightly accordingly, but instead one of the estate cars was waiting when she reached the front drive, an estate worker leaning against the driver's door talking to Luciano, who was loading his bag into the boot. Luciano looked up as Liv walked down the Castello steps and onto the drive.

'Front or back?' he asked.

'Depends on how long we are travelling for,' she said cautiously.

'Just to the train station. It's quicker to get the high-speed train to Naples than to fly.'

'Sounds good. In that case I'll be fine in the back.' She smiled her thanks at the driver as he took her bag and loaded it into the boot and she took her place in the back seat, careful not to touch Luciano, to act like the colleagues they were while here in the Castello.

It wasn't a long journey to the train station, where Liv found herself skipping the queues and ushered through to an airy and luxurious lounge before boarding the high-speed train in the first-class carriage which Luciano had somehow secured just for them. How he had managed it with such short notice she didn't know, and charmed by the luxury she sat back in the comfortable seat, accepted a glass of wine from the attendant and watched the Italian countryside fly by. There was so much of the country to explore! So much of the world. She had hinted at travelling to her mother, idly considered it in the brief moments she considered the future, but as the train took them at high speed through the country she made a decision. She had savings, she had a tenant, there was nothing to stop her.

'Carpe diem,' she murmured almost defiantly, as if trying to convince herself, waiting for excitement to engulf her now she had finally made a plan. But instead her gaze fell on Luciano, who was frowning at his laptop and it was as if her heart was being squeezed, a physical pain at the thought of moving on. She was the one who had insisted on short term and no feelings from the start, and it had been the right thing to do, the safe thing to do. She had to protect her heart, look to the future. But for one self-indulgent moment she allowed herself to imagine a different outcome, one without a time limit and a certain ending, before ruthlessly turning her attention back to the landscape. Feelings and daydreams would only lead to hurt; the only person she could rely on was herself.

Luciano worked for the whole journey and after a while Liv did the same, but it was hard to attend to emails and to-do lists when there was so much to see and as the train entered Rome, she gave up on any pretence of paying attention to her laptop, captivated by the snapshot of the eternal city visible through the window. A brief stop and then on again, south.

It was late afternoon when they reached Naples, the heat and colours and noise almost overwhelming, a stark contrast to the green peace of Tuscany. Liv had been warned about pickpockets and she kept her bag close as a porter collected their cases and strode on ahead. Feeling a little like Alice thrust into Wonderland she was grateful when Luciano took her arm and steered her through the crowds and out of the station to where another car awaited them. A short drive took them through the vibrant city before they drew up at the docks. A smart young man in blue shorts and a white polo shirt was there to greet them as Luciano opened her door and helped her out.

'I forgot to ask,' he said. 'Are you a good sailor?'

'I'm not sure,' she admitted. 'I've not done much sailing if I am honest.'

'Then let's find out.'

Their bags were being loaded onto a sleek boat and Luciano helped Liv aboard before springing onto the boat himself. The young man started to unwind various ropes while another man in the same uniform started the engine and within minutes the boat was heading out of the harbour and into the sea. She stood gazing at the blue waters, at the cloud-free sky and inhaled.

'I can't believe I am here,' she said as the wind started to whip her hair into a tangled mess.

'No regrets?'

'Not yet. Let's see how the sea sickness goes!'

*No*, Liv thought as Luciano slipped his arms around her waist and she leaned back into him. She would allow herself no regrets, not yet. Tomorrow might be a different matter but that could take care of itself.

* * *

The Isla Bella was the largest of three small islands close to Positano on the Amalfi Coast and had belonged to Luciano's family for several generations, the villa falling into disrepair until his grandfather's time when the whole had been renovated, his grandparents eventually spending half the year there as Luciano's father took over the estate and vineyard. Luciano had visited for large parts of the holidays when he was a boy, using the long summer days to sail, swim and paint. They were some of his happiest memories, which was why he still kept the island despite being too busy to visit often. The moment of anticipation as the island came into view never got old and he felt his gut tighten in response as the boat rounded the headland, the island finally visible.

'Just look at this coastline,' Liv breathed as she stood next to him on the deck. 'It's utterly glorious.'

One of the things he had always liked about Liv was her appreciation for beauty, whether art or landscape, food or experiences, the way her whole body seemed to light up with pleasure. She was practically vibrating with excitement as the boat neared the island's jetty, peppering him with questions. Yes, other family members used the island; no, he didn't rent it out; yes, it was safe to swim; yes, you could easily sail to any of the towns on the coast; no, it never felt isolated. Yes, it was magnificent in winter. The island felt new to him through her excitement, and he was glad of the impulse that had led him to suggest the trip. He was long overdue a visit and even if it didn't make sense for Liv to accompany him given their pact of secrecy, he knew he didn't want to leave her behind. Fate had given them a second chance at a summer romance; it would be churlish of him not to take ruthless advantage.

It was still light as the boat pulled in at the dock, a small natural harbour on the south of the island. Luciano grabbed a rope, ready give the deckhand a hand as the helmsman brought the boat alongside the jetty. Luciano jumped onto the jetty, rope in hand, and began to secure the boat.

'Welcome to La Isla Bella,' he said once he was sure the rope was securely tied, extending a hand to help Liv ashore.

If showing Liv the island from the sea had been exhilarating, showing her in person was ten times so from the paths cut into the cliffs to the sea water pools, different depths depending on their positioning, from the terraced gardens to the villa itself, positioned to face towards Positano, huge glass doors leading out from the main living area onto a sweeping terrace, incredible views in every direction, where a table was set for two. Once they had deposited their bags and Liv had time to tidy her hair, they took their seats at the table.

The sun was sinking now, tracing a fiery path along the sea, the horizon a kaleidoscope of colour. Maria, the housekeeper, had prepared a simple supper of fresh fish and aromatic salads, of local gelato served with fruits. The wine was perfectly chilled, the conversation easy and wide ranging, history and mythology, stories of holidays past. Liv might not want to work as a lawyer but Luciano could see how in the right job she would be a good one with her eye for detail and talent for questions.

'Were you ever lonely as a child?' she asked, as they took their drinks over to a comfortable outdoor sofa and settled into the warm August night air, Positano a blaze of light on the shoreline opposite. 'You were what, ten, eleven when Elisabetta was born? How old were you when your parents split up?'

'Eight. But it wasn't a shock when they did. In many ways they were never really together even when still married. My father liked the Castello, the vineyards, a simple life, whereas my mother liked cities and culture and being surrounded by people telling her how beautiful she was. She was, is, very beautiful.'

'Has she remarried?'

'Several times, no more children though. She didn't really take to motherhood. Even now she's happy for our relationship to be an annual dinner somewhere, which is more about being seen than the food and intimacy.' Lucian realised with a shock that there was a bitter tinge to his voice, a tinge he had spent his life trying to purge. His mother had made it clear she didn't want to be involved with his upbringing, so why would he give her any headspace? 'But no, I was a solitary child but not a lonely one. I had the vineyard, the people who worked there, my father and later Meg. My grandparents here. The deckhands who taught me to sail, the people who taught me about wine. My art. In many ways I was very privileged.'

'In many ways,' she repeated but her gaze was warm, empathic and Luciano got the sense he wasn't fooling her. How much had he shared with her on those long-ago Florentine nights when he had been younger and more impetuous, unshaped by the responsibilities he now bore?

'It must be very different growing up as the youngest child.' It was easier to turn the tables on her than continue with the introspection.

'The cliché is that the youngest child is the spoilt baby. It was a cliché my parents worked very hard to dispel. My siblings were so perfect it was inevitable in some ways I would be a disappointment.'

'I don't think you are a disappointment. I think they just worry about you.'

'No,' she sighed. 'I was a bit. You've met Portia and Max, they were just like they are now. The epitome of high achievers. They were both effortlessly top of the class, school prefects and head boys and girls and on every sports team imaginable. They took on leadership like it was their God-given right. I wasn't *not* academic, but I had to work harder for it. I was also arty and bookish and liked hanging out in malls trying on lip glosses with my friends discussing our crushes on One Direction.'

'*All* of One Direction?' he teased, enjoying her flush of embarrassment.

'Maybe—no judging, please! When it came to my interests my family just didn't understand me even though I am totally ordinary. They enjoyed debates and strategy board games and long competitive cycle rides and I didn't mind those things but in moderation. I just never had their drive to win.'

'I don't think you are ordinary,' he said, his voice low. 'Not at all. I think you are extraordinary.'

Her cheeks reddened. 'You don't have to say that.'

'I mean it.'

'Anyway, I am definitely disappointing and worrying them now. For me to have been let go from my job, to have no plan for what happens next, it terrifies them. And I *am* sorry for that. But I need to find out who I am when I don't have their voices in my head dictating the sensible path.'

'It's important to you? To find yourself?'

Liv laughed. 'You make me sound like some kind of hippy out travelling the world. But yes, I suppose it is. Doesn't everyone want to find out who they really are and what makes them happy?'

'I am glad Elisabetta is,' he said slowly. 'I want her to have that freedom. But I don't need or want to seek out my secret regrets or desire. I did what was right and that's what matters.'

'No matter what the cost?'

It was his turn to laugh. 'Look around you, Liv. I am hardly suffering.'

'No. But you do deserve happiness, Luciano. Don't forget that.'

'What do you deserve, Liv?'

'Me? I don't know about deserve but what I want…' She paused and took a sip of her wine, gazing out to sea, her expression a little wistful. 'I think for myself it's to find something, somewhere that feels right, you know? To find my own path, not trying to make myself fit into someone else's template of how life should be. And although I don't agree with my mother, I don't think settling down and marriage is necessarily the only sensible way to be, but I would like to meet someone one day who makes me happy. But I know better than to seek validation through someone else. I need to really be comfortable in my own skin before that can happen.'

Lucianio's hand tightened around his wine glass. Of course Liv deserved happiness and of course that would probably at some point involve some kind of romantic attachment. He just didn't want to think about her with anyone else, to imagine someone else touching her, kissing her, making her blush, eliciting the little gasps she made when he found her most sensitive areas. He inhaled, long and deep, pushing the unwanted image of her with an anonymous man away.

'I think you are being hard on yourself here. To me you are already there, you are forging your own path, taking a knock-back that might have felled someone lesser and creating an opportunity out of it. You might not know what comes next but you know what you *don't* want and you won't settle for convenience or money or making someone else happy at the expense of your own fulfilment. That's admirable. You have a lot of integrity, Liv.'

She blinked. 'Luciano. I think that's the nicest thing anyone has ever said to me.'

Slowly, deliberately, she put her glass down on the low coffee table and stood up, walking towards him. She wore the crumpled dress she had travelled in, her hair tied up in a loose knot, her face make-up free, and she was utterly beautiful. Liv reached him and took his glass from him, setting it next to hers with deliberate intent, before taking his hand and pulling him unresistingly to his feet, reaching up to cup his face with her hands.

'You always make me feel seen,' she said. 'You always did. That's what makes you so very dangerous, Luciano Del Visconti. Dangerous and irresistible.' And with that she stood on her tiptoes and kissed him.

Luciano pulled her close, deepening the kiss, the only sounds the roar of the sea matching the roar of his blood. *Mine*, his body whispered, as he ran his hands slowly up her back. *Mine.*

Luciano couldn't pinpoint when the shift had been but there had been one. Liv was no longer just an object of fantasy, a memory of more-innocent times or the bright, desirable woman whose presence lit up the Castello, but someone, something infinitely more dangerous. She had become a woman of possibilities, a woman who mattered to him, whose happiness mattered, whose presence mattered. But she was a woman unfinished, a woman who needed to figure out her path, and he was a man whose path had been determined for him and there was no deviation allowed. Fate might have reunited them but fate was known to be a cruel mistress and Luciano didn't need a crystal ball to know that the happiest ending they could expect was a pain-free parting and some good memories. So let them make those memories, starting with here, tonight, with a star-strewn sky and the ocean all around and the kind of kiss that only led in one direction.

With a muttered growl he picked her up, not breaking the kiss as he carried her over to the double sunbed on the edge of the terrace, depositing her on it. He stood there and looked at her, her eyes luminous, her lips parted, her hair falling out of the knot, and imprinted the picture firmly in his mind.

'Are you going to stand and stare or are you going to join me?' Liv asked, her voice husky.

'Oh, I can do both,' Luciano promised, his voice full of promise. 'What's the saying, good things come to those who wait?'

'How about even better things come to those who have no intention of waiting?' she asked, sitting up and unbuttoning her dress until it slid off her shoulders. She didn't take her eyes off Luciano as she unhooked her bra, letting it fall onto the bed beside her, shimmying out of her dress, her body outlined by the moonlight.

His blood raced as she smiled provocatively up at him. 'I think it's time we test that theory.' He discarded his own clothes in record time, joining her on the bed and claiming her with a kiss, primal and urgent, until he forget everything but her.

# CHAPTER EIGHT

LIV STRETCHED, REACHING out automatically, only to find the space beside her empty. Blinking to clear her sleep-filled vision, she peered round the semi-dark bedroom but could see no sign of Luciano. Flopping back onto the cool pillow, she allowed herself the luxury of a doze. She had no idea what time it was, but it didn't matter.

Time seemed different on this island idyll, every day a new adventure whether sailing out to explore private beaches and inlets across the coast, returning for dinner at a gorgeous restaurant in Positano or heading over to Capri for sightseeing and some of the best food Liv had ever tasted. She had spent a day in the natural spas and springs of Ischia feeling like a pampered princess, then yesterday a very different day, a sobering but fascinating one, walking the ancient streets of Pompeii. It was difficult to look at the volcano dominating the bay without a sense of unease after that, no longer a curiosity but a thing of horror and destruction. But having spent a few days on the gorgeous Amalfi Coast, Liv understood why people stayed here despite the risk. The rich volcanic soil was responsible for the delicious wines and mouth-watering fresh food, the seas for the incredible sea food, while the coastline looked like it had been designed by the gods for sheer pleasure. And sheer pleasure was exactly what she had been experiencing. In and out of bed. She shivered at the memory of exactly what she had experienced last night, and again in the early-morning light. Her dating history might have been patchy but she had had good sex before, enjoyable sex, but nothing this intense, this addictive, had never been so constantly turned on, just the brush of his hand against hers weakening her knees and making her stomach contract. She lay there for a few seconds longer, lingering on some particularly pleasant memories of the night before, until she reluctantly decided she really should get up.

Pulling on a pair of silk pyjama shorts and a matching vest, Liv paused long enough to run a comb through her hair, splash her face with water and quickly clean her teeth before wandering out of the spacious master bedroom suite into the even more spacious villa beyond.

It still seemed incredible that she was staying here, with her pick of three natural swimming pools to swim in and two little beaches to sunbathe on or swim from, several terraces to enjoy, staff on hand to whip up everything and anything her taste buds fancied, to say nothing of the gorgeous gardens and wilder parts of the island she could wander in, the peaceful courtyard garden and the insane views from every conceivable direction. The whole island was a paradise. Even her family had been impressed when she sent photos and videos of the island and coastline. Only Max had pried into the status of her relationship with Luciano; the rest of her family seemingly buying her story that she had been offered the use of the villa as a bonus. On the one hand it was a little insulting that they didn't consider that a gorgeous, rich, eligible Italian could be interested in her romantically. On the other it was a relief. She was struggling to define their friends-with-benefits arrangement to herself let alone to anyone else.

They *were* friends; she was pretty sure of that. They had their shared history, experiences and conversations that went well beyond the employer and employee. And there were definitely benefits. It was all good. Only…

Only, when she was alone, when she fell into an introspective mood like this, it was easy to get hung up on details. To question them. Details like the way her breath left her body when she saw Luciano. How much she liked it when he touched her, not just like *that*, although she liked that very much, but casually, a hand on her back, a touch on her arm. How she liked the way he smiled at her, the break from his usual solemn expression, the warmth and liking in his eyes directed at her.

She liked the rich timbre of his voice, the way his accent rolled over her name, making the one syllable substantial. She liked the way everyone who worked for him clearly valued and respected and worried over him. She liked the sure way he handled a boat, the cleanness of his dive and his strong, sure cut through the water. She liked the way he studied a menu with intent, the serious discussions with waiters and sommeliers whether they were in a Michelin-starred restaurant or a tiny cafe in a square somewhere. She liked the way he had guided her through Pompeii yesterday, never mansplaining, but giving her all the tools to understand the history for herself.

She had been besotted with the boy she had known in Florence. She was falling head over heels with the man she was getting to know all over again.

Liv sucked in a breath. There, she had named it, named the feeling that had haunted the last few days. No wonder she didn't want to explain the friends-with-benefits to anyone. Quite apart from it being the kind of excruciating conversation she would never have with her parents if she ever wanted to face them again, she had broken the rules, broken their contract.

Feelings were not supposed to be involved in this situation; she wasn't supposed to be falling for him. She just wasn't sure how to make it stop.

Liv stepped out on the terrace, breath stuttering as she caught sight of Luciano. He must have been for a swim, hair wet and slicked back, a few drops of water still glistening on olive skin, a linen shirt pulled on over his trunks. He was drinking coffee and seemingly intent on his laptop, but he looked up as she stood there, his half smile teasing. Liv suddenly felt shy. Uncertain.

'Ciao, sleepyhead.'

'What time is it?'

'Nearly ten. Would you like coffee?'

'Please.' Liv sank into the seat opposite. 'I can't remember the last time I slept in so late.'

'You're on holiday, remember?'

'True.' Liv accepted a coffee from Maria with a grateful smile and looked around. 'Another gorgeous day, what shall we do? It's our last day tomorrow so we need to make the most of it.'

'I have a few ideas.' Lucian's gaze swept her up and down meaningfully and Liv felt her cheeks heat up. 'We could take the boat out? You haven't been to Amalfi itself yet. How does spending some time at sea before heading to Amalfi for some sightseeing and dinner sound?'

'Let me think.' She pretended to ponder. 'Okay, that sounds acceptable.' Acceptable! How spoiled was she? 'What time do you want to set off?'

His gaze swept over her again. 'Oh, there's no hurry. How about lunchtime?'

'Not for a couple of hours?' Was that her voice, so breathless? 'What do you want to do until then?'

'I'm sure we can find a few ways to fill our time.'

'Really? Like what?' Liv stood up and

walked slowly over to the balcony, her hips swaying, aware that Luciano was watching her intently. She turned and looked at him, enjoying the appreciation in his eyes.

'I like this outfit on you,' he said. 'You should always wear little silk vest tops and shorts, I think. It's the way the straps slither off your shoulders.'

'Slightly limiting for most social occasions.' She knew she looked good, her usual pale skin tanned enough to highlight the cream, the silk clinging in all the right places. She sauntered slowly back to the table, where Luciano had turned his chair to face her. She stopped in front of him and he reached out to clasp her hips. She could feel his touch burning through the cool of the silk.

'But what I like most about this particular outfit,' he said, eyes dark as night, 'is how easy it is to peel off you.'

'Really?'

He nodded, his hands splaying, his thumbs brushing the bottom of her breasts. Her nipples hardened and heat flared in his eyes. 'Just a tug here…' He pulled the waistband of her shorts, sliding them down just an inch. 'Or here…' He bared one of her shoulders.

She swallowed. 'I am beginning to see what

you mean, but I think I need you to demonstrate a little more.'

Luciano's mouth curved and in one smooth move he was on his feet. 'I would be delighted.' He took her hand in his and led her through the villa and back to the bedroom. The bed was still unmade, the sheet thrown back, the curtains still drawn. He closed the door behind them and let go of Liv's hand, turning to face her, his expression full of intent.

'Are you ready for the demonstration?'

Liv licked her suddenly dry lips, aware he was watching every move, and nodded. 'Show me,' she said. 'And Luciano? I can be a slow learner. You may need to show me more than once...'

Luciano flicked open the menu but his eyes moved over the words unseeingly. It had been a perfect day. The kind of morning every day should start with. Sometimes Luciano couldn't believe that this was real, that this gorgeous woman was in his bed, by his side. That they had been given this second chance to finish what they started all those years ago. The very act of knowing there was an end date made the whole affair sweeter still, no worrying that it would peter out into arguments and miscommunication and the effortless suddenly a burden. Although at the same time, he was glad that the end date was still months away. He wasn't ready for that civilised goodbye just yet.

Not that it was inevitable for all relationships to end, obviously. Proof of that was all the weddings at the Castello, as was the handful of Luciano's friends starting to announce engagements or babies. They were still the minority but an increasing one.

Or look at his father and Meg. A true love story if ever there had been one. One that had started with a temporary contract and grown into a lifetime commitment. Had they known from the start that was where they were heading or had they too told themselves their relationship was fleeting?

'You look thoughtful.' Liv took a sip of wine, her gaze steady on him. 'Are you fixating on work or trying to decide whether this time you really can fit in that traditional pasta course between your antipasto and main course?'

'Definitely not the latter and actually not the former. No, I was thinking what a nice day it's been. It's a shame every day can't be like this.' It was true, if not the whole truth.

'It has been lovely, hasn't it? I hate that tomorrow is our last day. I wish we could stay forever. Do you think we'd get bored eventually if every day was sailing and sightseeing and many-course dinners?'

'That's not all this day included.' He grinned meaningfully at her. 'I very much liked the way it started too.'

She set her glass down demurely. 'With coffee and emails. That's standard, isn't it?'

He grinned. 'Any day that starts with Maria's excellent coffee is a good day.'

One of the things he had always liked about Liv was the way she teased him, the lack of ceremony. Growing up as the Del Visconti heir and then catapulted into being in charge so young, he was used to a certain amount of deference, of people wanting to be with him, near him, for *who* he was, not *what* he was. Liv had never stood on ceremony with him; nor did she now he was technically her boss. Nor did she take it for granted that because she was his guest he covered everything; she tried—and occasionally succeeded—to pay for their meals, for their gelato when out and about, the entrance to the villa on Capri or

Pompeii. Luciano wasn't used to being paid for. It was both nice and disconcerting but his efforts to stop her had ended with her telling him not to be a chauvinistic dinosaur. He liked that independence.

The waiter came over to take their order and the next couple of minutes were taken up with ordering before Liv turned back to him. 'So, you are telling me you were staring at the menu for five minutes with your brow furrowed because you have had a nice day? Interesting.'

'I wasn't just remembering the day, no, I was also thinking about my father and Meg.'

Her expression clouded. 'I'm sorry, I didn't mean to pry.'

'Not at all.'

'Do you want to talk about it? Tell me to butt out if not!'

Did he want to talk about it? Probably not. There was nothing *to* talk about, but the words spilled out almost unconsciously. 'I was just wondering when it started.'

'When what started?'

'Their relationship. I think I was a particularly unobservant boy so, to me it made sense. Meg arrived and then she stayed. But all along she was only planning to be there for a few months and then move on. At some point there must have been a first kiss, a decision to start something more. The decision to stay…'

Was Liv drawing the parallels he was? A young woman coming into the Castello for just a short while, a romantic situation developing. Two generations, two similar relationships but two different outcomes. Was that because his father and Meg had more courage? No, there was courage in his and Liv's situation too, in understanding and naming all the reasons they couldn't, shouldn't expect more, in negotiating a mutually agreed end point.

Liv folded her hands and rested her chin on them, regarding him thoughtfully. 'I guess they kept that part from you, were trying to be discreet and that's to their credit. No one ever likes to think about their parents' relationships, do they? I mean, I know mine met at Cambridge, that Mum was the northern working-class girl with a chip on her shoulder and more ambition than everyone else put together and Dad was the nice tennis-playing middle class boy who had been to an expensive school and followed well-travelled routes to the same college his father and grandfather attended. They were so different it's hard to see how they got together. It would have seemed more obvious that they hated each other. Perhaps they did at first, the classic enemies to lovers. But we've never asked. Maybe I will.' She laughed. 'Although Mum would probably tell me I am being ridiculously sentimental.'

'I don't know, I saw them dance at your brother's wedding. I think there is still some sentimentality there. You should ask them.'

'One day, when Mum isn't stressing about my lack of career I will. So what made you think about your father and Meg?' Liv's tone was casual, but Luciano couldn't help note that there was a peculiar tension to her shoulders, the way she focused on her fork rather than look at him.

It was the same tension, almost an introspection, he had noted in the morning after they had boarded the boat and sailed off. Liv had been quieter than usual, inward for a while although after a while she had seemed to shake whatever was worrying her off and revert to her usual bright self.

'I'm not sure,' he said slowly. 'I know they used to come here a lot, sometimes with Betta and I but often alone, it was their recharge place. It's inevitable I would think about them here, I suppose. It's just hit me how little I know about those early days. Which is why you should ask your parents while you can. That family history is important.'

He didn't want Liv to also draw parallels between their fling and his father's relationship. She might think he was hinting for her to revise her plans, asking her to stay and of course that wasn't the case. Hadn't he just been reminding himself how perfect it was that this, whatever it was, could exist in a bubble, unburdened by reality? A start, a middle, an end. Just a shame the end was rapidly approaching, the days slipping through their fingers. He needed to recentre himself. Remind himself what this was. Summer fun, no strings, no ties, no regrets. That this was what they both wanted.

Luciano leaned back. 'I needed this week, these last few weeks, more than I realised. It's been good to feel so carefree. And I have you to thank for that. These last few weeks, with you, with no plans, no promises, just the freedom to be ourselves, realising that not everything has to be a plan or a big deal. It can just be. You have inspired me.'

'Me?' Liv looked surprised. 'How?'

'Your bravery to face the world with no plan and see what comes next, your capacity to enjoy the moment. I can't do that too much, too many people rely on me. But I am learning that I am not responsible for everything and everyone all the time. Elisabetta doesn't need me the way she used to, in fact it's important she is more resilient. I am realising I can take time off, that I can even switch off sometimes. I am not sure I would be here right now without you. So thank you.'

Liv flushed. 'I think you are overstating any impact I have had but you are welcome. I just think I was in the right time at the right place. You and your sister were obviously ready for some changes. If I am being brutally honest I *am* a little scared about what comes next, which is why it's been brilliant to have these months here as a stopgap. Don't get me wrong, I'm excited too, but scared in case I get it wrong. These second chances don't come around often. I don't want to blow mine. Sometimes…' She stopped and took a sip of wine, not meeting his gaze.

*'Si?'* Sometimes what? It was like she had read his mind, realising how quickly time was slipping through their fingers. What would he do if she suggested staying in Italy, at the Castello a bit longer? Elisabetta had shown she didn't need him so much, and the business

was in a good place. *He* was in a good place. And he liked Liv, really liked her. Wanted her, enjoyed her company, couldn't get enough of her. But on the other hand, he was still trying to figure out what his life looked like with this new freedom Elisabetta's leaving had granted him. Did he want to swap one commitment for another so soon? Liv wanted to find her path; he had no idea who he was when all his responsibilities were stripped away. He needed to find out.

'Sometimes I like the idea of being the kind of carefree person who just leaves here and sees where the wind takes her but then I panic. Impulsivity led me here and that's worked out okay but it doesn't mean it's necessarily the template for the rest of my life. What if I get on a plane to…to… Buenos Aires but have the wrong clothes? Or don't have the right injections? Or the right visa?' She laughed. 'See, not that carefree after all. I hope you are not too disappointed in me.'

'You could never disappoint me.' Luciano had meant the words to be flirtatious, but they came out with an almost embarrassing intensity. He caught himself quickly. 'It's the willingness to change your life that's admirable, how you do it is up to you.'

It was a relief when the waiter interrupted them with their antipasto, a mozzarella-and-tomato salad for him, garnished with fresh basil, and prawns grilled to perfection for Liv. They smiled their thanks as the dishes were put in front of them and the wine replenished.

'What about you?' Liv asked once the waiter left. 'Your life has changed somewhat too. What will you do if October comes and your sister still hasn't returned?'

'Practically, look for another replacement. Emotionally? Be glad that she is out there finally living her life.'

'Personally?'

'I can't make a big change like you, Liv, and nor do I want to. Inheriting when I did was a burden, I have never denied that. But I know now, much as I am enjoying painting again, making a living from art was always an unachievable dream and I would have realised it eventually. For now small steps. More time here, allow myself to enjoy life more. Take a holiday, see an opera, small things.'

'Sounds good.' She held up her glass. 'Here's to change, however it takes us.'

Luciano mirrored the toast. 'To change. The one constant.'

It was a good thing she was moving on.

Liv needed to discover just what it was she wanted out of life and he had to discover how to make the most of *his* life. Once again fate had pulled them together at the wrong time. But that didn't mean they couldn't, shouldn't enjoy every moment they had left. He would miss her when she left but he wouldn't allow the now to be tainted by those fears; they were for another day. The future could take care of itself.

# CHAPTER NINE

'You look different. Have you grown your hair?'

Liv paused at Luciano's office door as she heard voices from within, a vivacious female voice chattering in Italian. She took a cautious step back but Luciano saw her through the open door and gestured for her to come in.

'Liv, come say hi to Elisabetta. Betta, this is Liv, who has kindly stepped in to manage everything which has made this trip of yours possible.'

Liv headed around to the other side of the desk and waved at the vivacious-looking girl whose face filled the screen.

'*Buongiorno*,' she said. 'Or is it day where you are? Where is that exactly?' It was hard to tell from the backdrop, which seemed to be an incredibly untidy bedroom. Having inherited the chaotic office, Liv could believe that the bedroom was Elisabetta's own.

'New Zealand,' Elisabetta said.

'How long have you been there?'

'Just a few days. I hadn't really planned to visit but Luc made a big deal of how I should spend time with my mother's family and so here I am.' The younger woman rolled her eyes at Luciano.

'New Zealand is meant to be beautiful,' Liv said diplomatically. 'Where else have you seen? It's been what, four months since you headed off?'

'About that. Let me see, I spent three months in Southeast Asia, have you been? Oh, you should,' she said as Liv shook her head. 'It's so beautiful and every country was so different and inspiring, you know? And the food! I was at a friend's yoga retreat in Thailand and then she and I did some backpacking around Thailand, moving on to Vietnam and Cambodia before heading to Bali for some fun because all that travelling got a bit intense, you know?'

'It must have.' Liv tried not to smile at the thought of needing a break from a break.

'Then I spent a few weeks in Australia, which was crazy fun, we had the best time. My friend is staying on there with family so I left her and headed to New Zealand and that's where I am!'

'Impressive.' Intense or not, travelling clearly suited Elisabetta. There was no trace of the anxiety Luciano had described, her eyes bright, her tanned skin glowing, the words falling out at pace as she described her adventures.

'Luciano said you are planning to travel too. I can give you lots of tips.'

'That would be great. I'm not going straight away though. I haven't had time to organise anything so am planning to head back to my parents' first to get things in order.'

Luciano shot her a quick look. She hadn't had an opportunity to communicate her plan to him. It was nice to see herself through Luciano's eyes, to think of herself as brave. But she knew she wasn't. A truly brave woman might have told Luciano what she was feeling for starters. That she wanted more than friendship no matter how good the benefits.

'Well, it was lovely to finally meet you,' she said to Elisabetta. 'I've heard a lot about you. Glad the travels are going well.'

'*Grazie*, and especially for stepping in,' the younger woman said. 'I know my filing system was a little…a little…'

'Idiosyncratic?' Liv grinned. 'Don't tell anyone but I quite enjoyed sorting it out. I'm not sure what that says about me. Ciao, Elisabetta.' She waved at the screen, smiled at Luciano and left the office, heading back to her own.

It was a very different space to the one she had inherited. The piles of papers had gone, all scanned and filed electronically as well as manually. She'd tidied away the many photos and pieces of art, many she recognised as Luciano's. It had felt too intrusive, looking at the memories of someone else's life. Now the room was uncluttered, clean. Almost impersonal. It was strange to think how at home she felt here, but when she left in just a couple of weeks all trace of her would be wiped as if she had never been. A sudden urge came over Liv to mark her presence in some way, to sign her name in a hidden corner, leave a framed photo of her somewhere, some proof of her presence. That she existed. Mattered.

'Idiot,' she muttered and opened her laptop.

She felt Luciano before she saw him, that sixth sense only he could provoke kicking in, and she looked up from her laptop to see him leaning against the wall. Her stomach dipped. God, he looked good. How did he seem to get more attractive every time she saw him, familiarity breeding lust?

'Hey. It was nice to see your sister. She looks so well.'

'*Si.* She does.' He didn't move and she raised her eyebrows.

'Are you coming in or would you prefer to loiter at the door?'

'I'm not disturbing you?'

'Always.' He was disruption in person, affecting her ability to think straight, the very molecules of her body. 'But I could do with a break. Compiling handover documents always take longer than you think, as soon as I think I have everything another twenty things occur to me.'

Luciano walked into the study, letting the door close behind him but he didn't sit down, pacing up and down for a few seconds until suddenly stopping in front of her desk.

'Why are you going back to your parents'?' His tone was abrupt. Almost accusatory.

*What on earth?* Liv sat back and looked up at him, trying to figure out what was bugging him, but his face was expressionless. 'Why am I going to my parents'? Because despite all my best intentions I haven't planned anything. I haven't booked a flight or applied for a visa or bought a rucksack. Like I said in Amalfi, there's a lot of planning that goes into being spontaneous. You know, I was sacked, let go, whatever, from law because all I wanted was some balance and then I came here and have had no balance at all. Now that, as Alanis Morissette would say, is pretty ironic.'

It really was. The difference was she didn't notice the time disappearing here, too caught up in the myriad and variety of things to do to bemoan her lack of free time. And any free time she did have she spent with Luciano, and there were definitely no regrets there. None apart from the hollow ache she felt whenever she remembered their time was finally running out.

'What about your flat?'

'Rented out, to that friend of Max's, remember?' Everything had fallen so nicely into place. Her pay-off money was tied up for a year, giving her a nest egg for when she returned to London, her flat let out, meaning that her mortgage and all the bills were being taken care of, and thanks to the aforesaid busyness she had barely touched the generous wages Luciano had paid her, wages she planned to use for her travel. Six months' travel, then a proper recalibration. A career that fulfilled her. Maybe even event planning full-time. It suited her and she was pretty good at it. But she wasn't rushing from one safe path to another, no matter how tempting it was.

And hopefully when she finally got started on this new phase she would look back on this time with Luciano and see it for what it was, a fling. No regrets, no wishing she had been bolder, had told him how she felt.

No missing him.

Maybe.

Luciano didn't look mollified, his brows drawn together, his mouth a thin line. 'I said you didn't need to leave the second your contract ended, that you could stay as long as you needed. You spent the whole of your brother's wedding trying to avoid your family, and now you are planning to live with them until you leave?'

Put like that it did sound like madness. 'It won't be for long, just a couple of weeks until I get sorted. They drive me crazy, and I know staying there will have its challenges.' That was an understatement if ever she had thought one. She laughed. 'Now Mum has accepted that this is happening she is trying to plan *for* me and Dad keeps sending me photos from his gap year. I think he wants me to follow in his footsteps no matter that half those countries don't even exist anymore. It's sweet really. Besides, I haven't seen them since June and if things go to plan, I'll be gone for at least six months. I *should* go home first and spend some time with them.'

'I don't disagree but I don't see why you need to do all your planning from there. There's no need to rush off, is there?'

'To rush off, no. But I do need to leave sooner rather than later.'

'But not straight away, surely? You could start your travels here. Things are quieter now the harvest is in and the events have stopped. Apart from the few days in Amalfi you have barely left the Castello. Stay longer and we could take some time to do all the things you haven't had time to do. Roma in autumn is very different to Roma in summer.'

It was a tempting thought. A boutique hotel, small intimate cafes and restaurants, iconic sites, more time with Luciano, acting like a couple. But that was the problem. It was all acting and at some point she needed to return to reality, before she started believing the fiction. 'I can't.'

'Why not? Unless...' He paused, expression tightening. 'Oh. How obtuse of me. We agreed on October as an end date, didn't we? I apologise, Liv. I didn't mean to push you into extending.'

Damn it, now he thought she was done with him, with them. She should allow him to think that. It was easier than admitting the truth.

Liv closed her eyes for a moment, trying to marshal her thoughts. Part of her wanted divert the conversation, to get up and walk over to him and kiss him until neither of them remembered what they had been talking about. But after all they had shared he deserved an explanation, her honesty.

'Say I stay. We spend more time together. What happens then?'

'We eat amazing food and drink amazing wines, we visit beautiful places and we make love.' He shrugged, his eyes gleaming with the intent which always made her knees weaken and her body heat up.

'That sounds incredible and it's not that I don't want to, it's just...' She bit her lip. 'It's just what happens when I fall even harder for you? How do I leave then? It's hard enough now knowing that in two weeks all this will be at an end, but extending that time will make leaving harder. I know this wasn't the deal. I know I promised just fun but it turns out there are things you can't legislate for and how I feel is one of those things.' Before she could stop herself she blurted out the words she had been so careful not to think let alone say. 'I think I fell in love with you eight years ago, Luciano, and being here again, being with you, I wonder if I ever really stopped. But you don't feel the same way.' It was a statement not a question. 'That's why I can't stay.'

Luciano always seemed so in control—out of the bedroom at least, but not now, staring at her in shock, obviously lost for words.

'Liv… I…'

'I thought not.' She tried to muster a smile. 'And that's fine. Obviously.'

But now she had said the words it wasn't fine, it wasn't fine at all.

Luciano stared at Liv, thoughts and emotions in such a tumult that as soon as one became clear another took its place. Horror that he hadn't expected this, sadness that he couldn't instantly tell her what she needed to hear and wipe that too bright smile off her face. A smile that didn't quite reach her eyes.

'I care about you, a lot.'

Ouch. He winced as he saw the words land, as Liv's expression shuttered.

'I like you, I am ridiculously attracted to you.' Wasn't that enough at this stage? 'But love? Liv, I don't know.' He had to be honest, with himself as well as her. 'I don't know what that means, what it is. What we have is amazing, why label it?'

'If you did you would know,' she said quietly. 'But honestly, Luciano, forget it. I shouldn't have said anything. I've ruined everything.'

'Don't say that. It's not you.'

She held up a hand, as if to ward his words off. 'Please, don't tell me it's not me it's you. I can cope with you not feeling the same way, but I can't hear that. I've used that line myself and it was *always* them.'

Luciano ran an exasperated hand through his hair. How had things turned so quickly? One minute he had been chatting to Elisabetta, delighted to see her looking so young and relaxed, like a gap year student not a preternaturally grown-up young woman with a dozen responsibilities on her slim shoulders. And then Liv had mentioned she was going back to England and he had felt…rejected. Which was ironic because this was clearly how she felt, on her feet now, body language defensive.

'I think it would be easier for us both if you

left,' she said, chin tilted. 'Please don't think you have to say something, I don't need platitudes. My feelings are my problem, not yours.'

Leaving felt wrong but it was what she had requested and reluctantly, he turned and stalked towards the door. He stopped when he reached it, wishing he could find the right words. But no matter how he grappled for them they wouldn't come and with a smothered curse he left her office.

The rest of the day passed in a blur. Luciano buried himself in work as he had so many times before. When the day ended, he started his usual path towards his studio but paused at the bottom of the staircase. Art meant introspection, emotions, searching for clarity, things he didn't want to face right now, so instead he made his way to the kitchen, and snagged a few beers and some bread and cheese, and left the Castello, his footsteps taking him unerringly to the orchard bench. The trees were turning, no longer green but rusts and coppers, gold and umbers, here and there leaves drifting to the ground. October. The harvest in, the grapes pressed, the miracle of turning the juice into wine starting down at the factory. The fields were harvested and resown, vines and olive trees pruned and prepared for the winter. Autumn was a time of activity, finishing the year's work, preparing for the next cycle. A time of bounty and celebration, the air cooler, the sun gentle, a stark contrast to the height of summer. Autumn usually brought relief, but not today.

Luciano sank onto the bench and opened a bottle of beer, taking a long deep swig, staring out over the hills. He was the product of a bad marriage and a good one, a distant family and a close one. He had spent the last eight years as brother, parent, confidant, guardian and caretaker and was only just emerging from the restrictions of that role, but freedom still felt elusive. Ephemeral. He didn't know *who* he was when he wasn't bearing all that responsibility. Once that hadn't mattered, he was needed too much, but now he really wanted to know. Had to know.

If he didn't know himself how could he know how he felt about another person? Spending time with Liv was exciting and fun, sensual and tender, freeing. He'd enjoyed the lack of responsibility, the freedom to just be. He'd thought she had to. That they wanted the same things. Yes, he had wondered *what if* at times but that was all it had been, a fleeting thought, a day dream. He hadn't realised that she wanted more, felt more. If he had he would have finished things, minimised the impact. At least he hoped he would, hoped that he hadn't seen the signs and ignored them, too focused on their pleasure to recognise any potential pain.

Regardless, now she was hurting and it was his fault. Again. No matter that he hadn't intended to hurt her then or now, the outcome was the same.

'I thought I might find you here.'

Once again it was inevitable that Liv would appear, a repeat of that very first evening. She came and sat down next to him and wordlessly he opened a second beer and handed it to her.

'Thank you.' She lifted the bottle and took a long drink. 'That's better.'

They sat in silence for a few minutes before she spoke again. 'Luciano, I'm sorry.'

He looked at her, surprised. 'Why should you be sorry? I'm the one who…'

'Because I threw something at you that you weren't expecting and then got upset when you didn't reciprocate the way I wanted you to. That was unfair. I shouldn't have told you what I was feeling. I knew you didn't feel the same way, that you weren't ready to hear it.' She winced. 'My new, impulsive live-for-the-moment creed is leading me astray already and I haven't even got started.'

Luciano couldn't let her shoulder the blame. 'This is on me, not you. The truth is I don't know *how* I feel. Liv, I have spent eight years *not* feeling. It was the only way I could get up every morning and do what needed to be done. I wanted to rage and grieve, for my Papa and for Meg and all the things they wouldn't get to do, to see. For Elisabetta and the way her life was destroyed. For my own selfish dreams and the changes I had to make. But I had to be strong and focused, always, and that meant not allowing any introspection, to do not be.'

'I know.'

'I dated a little, sometimes more than a little. But my head and heart were always here. The one time I went away for a couple of days with someone I had been seeing for a while Elisabetta called, she'd had a bad day and needed me, and I left. I wasn't very popular.'

The trace of a smile curved her lips. 'I can imagine.'

'And that was fine. Those relationships were nothing more than this,' he explained as he lifted the beer. 'A way to pass the time. And then Elisabetta left, you arrived, I started painting again. It felt, feels like I am discovering who I am again, who Luciano is, but I've only *just* begun that process. And it's painful and slow and difficult but I need to do it, because otherwise I will always be half here, always half in.' Did she understand? It was imperative that she did. 'It would be easy to say I love you, too easy, because you are incredible and I feel a lot for you. I like you, you make me laugh, I am in awe of your energy and organisational brain, I want you all the time. It would be easy to ask you to stay, to fall into a life with you. But I am still half formed, Liv. And I think so are you. You have dreams of your own that belong far from here, dreams I can't share with you because my life has to be here and that can't change. I don't want you to lose out on those dreams, and I need to spend some time learning who I am when all my roles have been stripped away.'

Luciano felt almost winded, the words torn out of him, words and feelings he had never allowed himself to articulate before.

'Our timing really sucks, doesn't it?' Liv said at last.

Luciano hadn't expected to laugh but the unexpectedness of her comment surprised him into one. 'It really, *really* does.'

She took another long gulp of her beer then

leaned against him, her head heavy on his shoulder.

'I wish I could say that you are wrong. Had some argument to show that we should be braver and bolder. To convince you that my feelings are real and that you feel the same way. But that wouldn't be fair on either of us.'

'I don't doubt you for a minute,' he said hoarsely. 'It took a lot of courage to say what you did, I appreciate it.' Such banal words for such strength of feelings. 'And you are probably right. When I figure things out I will probably curse myself for not realising just what we had and letting you go.'

In some ways he already was; he could feel her slipping away already, the certainty of them dissolving into something far more nebulous and it hurt, physically.

'Then you'll come after me, chase me to the end of the earth, ready to atone for your short-sightedness only to find me surrounded by adoring suitors?'

'I'd fight them all. But I can't now, Liv. Not yet.' He hoped, prayed she understood even though he barely understood himself.

She didn't answer for a bit and then she exhaled, a deep shuddering sigh. 'I know. I've always known. That was why we had the contract. Short-term, no feelings. I didn't mean to break it, to tell you that things had changed for me. But I think we have always been honest with each other and I didn't want to stop now. And you are right. We can't carry on a long-distance relationship for an unspecified amount of time with no end game. It wouldn't be fair to either of us, and much as part of me wants you to ask me to stay, if I did then I would be swapping one ready-made safe path for another, and look how the last one turned out. I don't want any regrets—and I don't regret spending the summer here. I've learned a lot about me, about what I want, what I don't want. How can I regret that?'

'So what now?' There were still two weeks to go, one last wedding, one walking party.

'I see through my commitments, then head home as planned.'

'And us? If you want to stop then I understand.'

'Maybe I should, it would be sensible, but I don't *want* to be sensible. I spent eight years doing that.'

She turned to him, eyes luminous in the moonlight, and not for the first time Luciano wondered what on earth he was doing. He should be on his knees begging her to stay, not rationalising why leaving was the right thing for them both. Instead he did the only thing he could do, cupping her face in both hands and kissing her, slow and sweet and tender at first and then with increasing intensity as she opened up to him, kissing her like it was the first time and the last time, like this was his only chance, the kiss saying everything that he couldn't articulate. Slowly, reluctantly he pulled away and stood, looking down at her for a long moment before extending a hand. 'Come with me? Please?'

Liv didn't answer but she stood up and took his hand, her fingers slipping between his as if they belonged there, and he led her back to the Castello. If two weeks were all they had then he needed to make the most of every second, starting right now.

# CHAPTER TEN

'Liv!'

'Hey, Max.' Liv peered into her phone, glad to see her brother's familiar grin. 'It is so good to see you.'

'Good to see you are alive and well. Look at you! So tanned! Mind you, you were still disgustingly tanned when you were home. Italy suited you.'

'Honestly I think Italy suits everyone. But I can't deny it's been nice following the sun. November in London was too cold for me and it turns out the January blues are a lot easier when the sun shines.'

'Rub it in, why don't you? Have you spoken to the parents recently?'

'Yesterday. They are really trying to be supportive, which is lovely but *you* know what their support is like.'

'Complete and utter takeover?'

Liv nodded. 'Mum has bought at least five

guidebooks and printed a dozen possible itineraries which she wants to chat through every time we speak. My whole *see where I want to go next* plan completely baffles her but she's trying. She and Dad have watched every episode of Race Across the World and taken notes on must-see sites and travel tips and she's mapped out volunteering opportunities in every country she's decided I should head to in an organised and timetabled manner. Meanwhile Dad has unearthed all these old photos from the attic and at any given moment is sending them to me waxing lyrical about the good old days when travelling meant turning up somewhere and hoping to find a bed with none of this internet nonsense and how amazing Thailand was before the rest of the world found it.'

Her brother laughed. 'I can just see it.'

'And then Portia and Celeste message me and they have clearly also got the *support Liv* memo. Celeste is obviously *totally* confused and thinks I need an intervention to get me back on track but she's trying, while Portia is treating me like I am liable to break at any moment. When I called her last week she used that special gentle voice she was using when I was back. I keep wanting to yell that I am having a year out not a terminal diagnosis although I suppose to Porsh, being sacked *is* a terminal diagnosis.'

'Can you imagine? The world would stop turning first. Anyway, enough about the family, let's focus on your favourite brother. Guess where I am.'

'The village pub?'

'How did you guess?'

'There is no way Annabel would allow that decor in the house. Besides I recognise it from the weekend I spent with you.'

Liv had enjoyed a weekend at Max and Annabel's house before embarking on her travels. They had settled in an idyllic village complete with a village green, duck pond and thatched-roof pub. November had been particularly cold, and frost still glittered on some of the rooftops and bare branches. It had been a complete contrast to autumnal Tuscany. As was her current location, predictably but enjoyably a beach in Thailand. It was beautiful, but it wasn't Tuscany.

No, she wasn't going to think about Tuscany. Not think about the moment her taxi had pulled up and she had said goodbye to Luciano, turning down his offer to drive her to the airport. She had needed that public, semi-formal goodbye.

Needed not to think about the two weeks between her awkward declaration and final parting. It should have been difficult, bitter-sweet or acrimonious somehow but it hadn't been. Instead there had been a new urgency to their love making. An understanding that this was all they had and therefore they needed to make the most of it. Liv had thought she might be broken-hearted when she left but there was a certain positivity in knowing that she was driving her own decisions. That she could have stayed longer but had chosen the end point. That she had been brave enough to lay her heart on the line. A positivity to owning her feelings, acknowledging that there was no blame here, just time and circumstance. It didn't mean that she hadn't shed a tear, more than a few. That she didn't lie awake at night wondering if things could have been different, missing Luciano. That she hadn't gone over every moment they spent together, reliving that first kiss, the last kiss.

A girl needed a certain amount of wallowing before moving on after all.

But not when she was on a gorgeous beach, with a snorkelling session planned.

'Ten points to the littlest Davenport. Annabel is hosting some of her friends so I jumped on my bike and came straight here. So,' Max asked. 'How's the nightlife?'

'I don't know,' she admitted. 'I haven't actually been out much.'

Her brother's expression softened. 'I know it's hard to put yourself out there, Liv, and you probably feel ancient compared to all those gap year kids but…'

'It's not that,' she said indignantly. 'I have made plenty of friends, thank you very much and not everyone is under twenty. I just haven't felt like it.'

She didn't want to tell him how tired she often was, that the smell of alcohol actually made her feel nauseous. Besides, she wasn't on *that* kind of gap year; she probably was too old for hedonism even if she *was* feeling up to it. Scenery and culture and experiences were what she was after, not shots and clubs.

'Well no wonder you look so healthy. You're glowing. But that might be the filter you've chosen. Speaking about glowing…' He paused and his cheeks reddened.

'What?'

'Annabel is also glowing.'

'That's nice.'

Max coughed meaningfully. 'She's *glowing*, Liv. Can you work out why?'

'She ate something radioactive? Spent too long on a sunbed? Oh!' She said as she realised what her brother was clumsily hinting at. 'She's pregnant? Oh my goodness, congratulations!'

'Thank you.' Max looked absurdly proud as if he had completed some terrifying quest as opposed to taking part in the easiest part in the whole baby-making process. Not that she wanted that image, thank you very much. 'She's due in June, we got the all-clear to tell people today and of course I wanted you to know straight away.'

'Thank you, wow! Pregnant! How exciting. How is she?'

'Amazing, you know Annabel. She felt a little nauseous. That was the first sign actually. The smell of alcohol and coffee made her ill and she was tired, which is so unlike her. Couldn't get up for her 6:00 a.m. yogalates. We weren't *trying* trying but not *not* trying if you get me.'

'Lalala. Honestly, Max. Can we at least pretend this is the work of a stork? I don't want to think about my brother in any kind of baby-making scenario that doesn't involve big birds carrying babies in their beaks, okay?' But even as she spoke Liv's brain was busily putting Max's words together.

Tireder than normal.

Couldn't abide the smell of alcohol.

Pregnant.

Surely not. Travelling was just playing havoc with her; that was all.

Only, when had she last come on? She had always been annoyingly irregular; it wasn't unusual for six weeks or even two months to go by before her next period. But she hadn't had one in November, *or* December and here they were in January.

January. Three months since she had left Italy. Three months since she and Luciano had last slept together.

No. She was catastrophising. It was impossible. Only, it *wasn't* impossible. Unlikely, but not impossible. No method apart from abstinence was one hundred per cent after all and they had been far from abstaining.

'Her breasts are getting bigger every day.' Max continued to rattle off TMI oblivious to Liv's internal panicked dialogue. She looked down at her own breasts. They *had* been a little tender, and yes, they looked bigger. 'It's fascinating. We are charting the size of the baby. It's the size of a plum!'

'A *plum*?' Liv put a hand on her own belly and tried to imagine a plum in there.

'One day it will be the size of a watermelon. Imagine!'

Liv didn't *want* to imagine, she didn't want to think about that at all.

Luckily Max didn't notice how distracted she was, too busy taking Liv through the pregnancy so far in exhaustive detail. All she was required to do was nod, smile and say 'Wow!' at various intervals until finally he rang off, leaving Liv to sit back in her hotel room and try to breathe.

When she had said she was going to spend time finding her path she had meant following well-trodden backpacker routes followed by a job that didn't make her want to scream at regular intervals, not get knocked up by the one who had got away. Got away twice.

Only she didn't actually know if she *was* pregnant. She was travelling, new foods, new places, different time zones, no routine. All the symptoms she was experiencing could be just as easily down to those reasons. First thing, establish the facts, there was time to panic later. She'd noted a pharmacy on the small high street and so Liv set out from her room, nodding blindly to a couple of acquaintances, promising to meet them on the beach later, barely noticing what she was saying.

Once in the pharmacy she stood still for what felt like hours, staring at the selection of pregnancy tests. She needed to know but at the same time she wanted to stay here for a little longer, stay in a world where nothing was confirmed and her only decision was how long she would stay at this resort and where she would go next.

It might have been two minutes or two hours later when she took the two boxes she had chosen over to the desk, avoiding eye contact as she paid for them, stuffing the package deep into her bag as she hurried back to her hotel room, barely noticing the stunning view from the small balcony or the laid back bohemian decor that had so charmed her when she had checked in. Instead she dropped her bag onto the bed and, with shaking hands, pulled out the two boxes. She wasn't sure why she had bought two, hazy memories of her friend's high school scare where they had hoped a different brand might change the outcome influencing her unconscious decision. Grabbing one at random, she took it into the bathroom, heart hammering.

Four tests and several bottles of water later there was no denying the facts. She was well and truly pregnant. As pregnant as her sister-in-law. Only she wasn't ensconced in a five-bedroom house in Surrey with an adoring spouse and well-paid maternity leave but unemployed, overseas and single.

She had wanted to change her life. Here was a lesson to be careful what you wished for.

Only… Liv put a hand on her belly. 'Sorry, little plum,' she said aloud. 'I've kind of messed this up, haven't I?'

Grabbing her sunglasses, she headed back out and made her way to the beach. It was like paradise, the sand white and fine, the sea impossibly blue. Liv kicked off her shoes and walked through the shallow water, the gentle waves lapping her ankles, and she tried to disentangle all her myriad emotions.

Panic, that was an obvious one, anger at being so stupid at her age to get caught out in this way. She was supposedly intelligent, nearly thirty and yet here she was in the same position Hetty Greene had been in back at school. But there was also an irrepressible joy, excitement. Because her situation might be far from ideal, but she couldn't deny she *was* excited. She might be unemployed but she was employable, she had savings and a flat. She might be single but she knew who the father was.

She stopped and touched her stomach again. A baby with Luciano's eyes.

Liv stared out to sea. There was no real doubt in her mind. She was going to keep the baby. It felt right. Like this was the path she had been searching for. It made sense in ways she couldn't articulate despite all the obvious downsides. But making that decision was just the start of many other difficult decisions, and top of that list was Luciano.

She couldn't *not* tell him. He had a right to know. But if the timing was bad for her, she knew it was catastrophic for him. He'd literally just got his life back, was still figuring out what that meant. So she needed to make it clear that she didn't need him to do anything he didn't want to do. That he could be involved as much or as little as he felt ready for. But even as she thought the words doubt crept in. He was Italian, with all the sense of pride and familial responsibility that meant. He saw it as his role to shoulder the burdens of everyone in his orbit. Once he knew about the baby there was no way he wouldn't insist on being fully involved, even if it wasn't what he wanted. Was telling him trapping him? And what would it be like raising a child with a man who she loved but who didn't love her?

She couldn't do this alone. Liv pulled her phone out of her pocket and found a contact and pressed it. It rang a few times and then a familiar voice.

'Olivia?'

'Mum?' To her horror, Liv felt her throat thicken. 'Mum, I need you.'

The Castello had never felt so empty. Which, considering the amount of staff employed there or based there, was ridiculous. But as the early-winter evenings drew in and they all left for their own houses and apartments leaving Luciano alone, he realised just how lonely his home could be. How much time he had in the evenings, time neither painting nor work could really fill. He slept fitfully, often waking up in the early hours, his bed too big, too cold. He had wanted time to think, to get to know himself. Turned out a man could have too much of a good thing. He had been using his time productively. Doing things, rediscovering all the things he had enjoyed when younger. Hiking, climbing, cycling, returning home exhausted physically and yet still unable to sleep, heading to his studio to fill the time to paint, abstract colours, bold and dark. But he still felt empty. Restless.

Some evenings he would take out his phone and hover over Liv's name, start to compose a message. A brief check-in. A friendly reach-out. But he always deleted them unsent. It would be unfair, selfish to disturb her. He had made his decision and he had to live with the consequences. And it had been the right one. She deserved to be living her best life, seeing the world, meeting people. Other men maybe. Men who could give her what she deserved. Men who were not afraid to feel.

'*Idiota*,' he muttered as unwanted scene after scene filled his head. Liv in clubs, dancing, hair streaming down her back, Liv on a beach hand in hand with some faceless man, Liv smiling at someone who wasn't him.

Luciano poured himself a glass of wine and carried it through to his study. He didn't use the room much in summer, preferring to be outside, but in winter it was cosy, a fire in the grate, books lining the walls, an armchair moulded to his shape. It was close to Elisabetta's room and so he used to work or read in here, keeping an ear out for her shouts, ready to soothe the night terrors that had plagued her for so long. But her room was empty; she had extended her visit to New Zealand, was talking about studying over there and he was delighted for her, he really was. But he missed her.

He missed Liv.

He took a sip of wine, his winemaking brain kicking in as he assessed the depth, the taste, the bouquet, and stared into the flames, startled by the vibration of his phone. Elisabetta. He accepted the call and smiled at the screen, hoping she wouldn't notice the shadows under his eyes.

'Hello, *cara*.'

'Are you sitting alone in the dark like a sad old man?'

'I am enjoying a glass of wine and the fire like a man who appreciates the finer things in life,' he replied with as much dignity as he could muster.

'Luc, it is Friday night. What are you doing sitting in alone? Why aren't you impressing some lucky girl in that sports car of yours? I always said it was wasted on you!'

'I've been working all day and…'

'Thirty-two going on eighty-two, that's you.

Do I need to come home and stage an intervention? Actually, what's the temperature?'

'It's been about five.'

'In that case I'll intervene from here. Summer in January is pretty cool. I went surfing today. Noah said I was getting really good.'

'Noah?'

'My surf instructor.'

'Do I need to come and check out this surf instructor?'

'Don't be so medieval. This is why you need a love life of your own to keep you out of mine.'

'Aha! So you do have a love life?' he teased.

'We are not talking about me.' Elisabetta paused and then said in a disinterested voice that showed she was very interested indeed. 'Have you heard from Liv?'

'No. Why?'

'I was just wondering how she was getting on. Did she go to Asia in the end?'

'I don't know.' He did not want to have this conversation but Elisabetta wasn't picking up on his tone. Actually, she probably was but was just ignoring it.

'Oh, I thought you might be planning a visit out to see her.'

'Why did you think that?'

'You two *were* together, weren't you?'

Luciano fought the urge to ask Elisabetta how she knew that. In the end Liv and he hadn't managed to maintain the secrecy they had agreed on. There had been no pda's or anything unprofessional, but even the most oblivious member of staff had realised that they were spending a lot of time together. In reality tongues had probably stated wagging when they had gone to the Amalfi Coast together. It was inevitable that the news would have reached his sister eventually.

'It wasn't serious.'

'But you like her?'

'Of course. What's not to like?'

'So what happened?'

'Nothing happened, Betta. Her contract came to an end, she had plans and she left. No big deal.'

Only it had been a big deal. Watching her drive away he had been conscious of a loss so profound it had hurt, of opportunities lost, of a second chance slipping through his fingers. But he hadn't done anything except stand and watch her go.

'Why didn't you go with her?'

He huffed out an exasperated sigh. 'We

can't all take off on a whim, Elisabetta. Someone has to be here to manage everything.'

She paled. 'I could have come back. You only had to ask.'

'I'm sorry, I didn't mean to snap. It's just not that easy. My life is here, Liv's isn't. So it doesn't matter how I feel.'

'It's my fault isn't it?' she said in a small voice and he stared at the screen in disbelief.

'What are you talking about, *cara*? Nothing is your fault except the state of your filing system.'

'I kind of took it for granted that you were always there for me. But you were so young yourself, not much older than I am now when you gave up everything for me.'

'Hey, less of the past tense. I am still young, thank you.'

'But you never got to *be* young. You couldn't even date because every time you did I ruined it. And now I am here and you are still stuck there and you have forgotten how to have fun and how to let anyone in.'

'What *have* you been reading? Have you been watching self-help influencers again? I know how to have fun.' But he wasn't sounding very convincing even to himself. 'I love the Castello, I enjoy making wine, I am painting again. I have everything I need. Please don't worry about me. I am glad you are seeing the world, that you are doing so much better. It's all I want.'

'But that's it. You should want things for yourself not me! You've been so busy looking out for me for all this time and putting yourself second I worry you've forgotten that *you* matter too. You like Liv, I know you do and you just let her walk away.'

'It's not that simple.'

'Maybe it should be.' Oh, to be twenty-one and to think liking and wanting was enough. 'At least tell her how you feel, Luc.'

'I don't *know* how I feel.'

Elisabetta laughed. 'You are many things, big brother, but you are not a liar or a coward. She is not going to travel forever, is she? It's not like she's been exiled to the other side of the world. And you *are* allowed to take a holiday. Go and see her. It doesn't have to be some big deep thing. Just be open to the possibility that she's good for you. Don't self-sabotage because you don't believe you deserve good things.'

'I don't think that!'

'No? Then prove it.'

Finally, the call ended, Luciano managing to

steer his sister away from the thorny topic of his love life or lack of it, but her words stayed with him. Was he self-sabotaging? Why had he been so quick to shut Liv down, to push her away? Why did he think that her life should be lived away from here? Was it because his choice had been taken away from him, that for all the money and prestige and the fact that he actually enjoyed his role, he had had no choice about it? Did the Castello subconsciously feel like a duty, one he didn't want to impose on anyone else? Because actually Liv had been happy here. Had come alive here.

And he had been happy too. She had brought colour and light and joy into his life, and he had sent her away without letting her know how much that meant, telling himself it was the unselfish thing to do when in reality he was just afraid. Afraid to let her in. Afraid to admit how much he cared. Because loss hurt. It was a vulnerability. It was safer to be alone. But she had allowed herself to be vulnerable. Had told him she loved him. How much courage had that taken? Courage he hadn't reciprocated. Not even in the safety of his own thoughts.

He looked at his watch. It was the middle of the night in Thailand, if that was where

Liv even was. Too late to call but he could message.

For the twentieth, fiftieth, hundredth time he typed out a quick message, but this time he pressed Send before he had the opportunity to talk himself out of it.

Ciao. Hope your travels are everything you wanted them to be, I just want you to know that I miss you.

It was the opening to a dialogue if she wanted one and if she didn't then that was on him. All he could do was wait. Luciano wasn't expecting to hear anything that evening and tried—and failed—to give his book his full attention, grabbing his phone the second it buzzed with a message.

It was from Liv.

Hope warred with anxiety as he opened it, fully expecting to read a message telling him to go away and never contact him again. Instead he read four short words.

We need to talk.

He frowned. That sounded ominous. Maybe she had met someone else, was engaged, married…

Of course, phone call?

In person might be better. I'm back in England. I'll come to you if that's okay?

She was back? She could only have been away a few weeks not months like she had planned. The unease intensified, was she ill?

When?

As soon as possible. I'll send you details.

Okay.

Luciano put his phone down and stared into the fire once again, unease turning to joy and back again. On the one hand he would see Liv again and very soon. This was his chance to put things right. To be honest with her and with himself. But on the other something was clearly wrong. The sooner she arrived and he found out what was going on the better.

# CHAPTER ELEVEN

LIV WAS A bundle of emotions when the taxi drew up at the Castello. The first was overwhelming relief. She felt like she was coming home in a way she had never felt before, not even over the last week ensconced in her childhood bedroom with her mother bringing her weak tea and toast for the nausea that had set in with a vengeance once she had arrived back in London.

Anticipation. She had missed Luciano. Fiercely. Physically and emotionally. Every sight, every taste, every experience she'd had while away she had wanted to share with him and it had taken all her self-control not to call and text him, to send photos, to keep those lines of communication open.

Dread. Because in an hour she would know if he was in or out. Oh, he would say he was in—she had no doubt about that—but she would know by the look in his eyes whether he really meant it or not.

'Remember,' her mother had said as she dropped Liv off at the airport. 'You have choices and those choices include a home with us for as long as you need.' Funny how it took a crisis for Liv to realise how much she still needed her mother sometimes, that her habit of taking control was sometimes exactly what was required. It was even funnier how much Liv's mother took her news in her stride. A job loss the end of the world, an unexpected baby a joy, no less wanted than Max and Annabel's, and yet always clear that whatever Liv did it was her decision, no pressure or recriminations.

Liv clambered out of the taxi and steadied herself, glad to be no longer travelling, even gladder that the nausea had, in the main, passed. As she straightened Luciano walked out of the front door and down the steps leading to the sweeping driveway.

'Ciao. I hope your journey went well.' Nothing in his tone or his eyes gave away his thoughts about her unexpected visit.

'Ciao,' she said, unexpectedly shy, her heart hammering at the sight of him, tall and solid and everything she wanted, needed. If only he felt the same way. *I'm not here to trap him*, she reminded herself. She just hoped he believed that. Besides, he had reached out first. She'd clung onto that thought throughout the flight. She'd still been trying to work out when and how to tell him when his text had arrived, unexpected and pushing her into action at last.

She'd travelled light with just an overnight bag, which he insisted on taking from her after he paid the taxi driver. Liv followed Luciano up the steps into the grand main hall, that feeling of coming home still prevalent.

'We have a couple of hours of daylight and it's not too cold today. Do you want a walk or are you too tired after your journey?' Luciano was being oddly formal. He hadn't touched her, hadn't even given her the usual Italian double kiss.

'That would be nice. I'm a little cramped so it would be good to get some exercise. Give me a couple of minutes to freshen up.'

It was absurd; they were acting like strangers, dancing carefully around each other. Liv splashed some water on her face, ran a comb through her hair and applied a little concealer and lip gloss before heading back to the hall where Luciano was pacing up and down. 'Ready?'

'Absolutely.'

It was no surprise that he led her through the gardens and up the path to the orchard. To the place where it had all begun and then ended. The air was cold but invigoratingly fresh, aromatically sweet, and Liv drew in gulps, letting it fill her lungs. 'I've missed this,' she said.

Luciano didn't reply. She'd expected him to ask her about her travels, ask why she was back in London, but he was silent, introspective. All small talk had fled from her brain too, the news she was about to impart so huge, so life changing, she was afraid if she said anything else she would just blurt it out, so she too stayed quiet, letting the green countryside replenish her soul. At last they reached the bench; neither sat, but stood beside it and gazed out at the views.

'I want to apologise,' Luciano said abruptly just when the silence had started to feel uncomfortable.

Liv gaped at him. 'For what?' Oh God, he didn't regret *them*, did he? Regret those four months that no matter what would remain some of the happiest in her life? That would make her impending announcement even more of a shock.

'When you told me you had feelings for me I panicked. I didn't know to respond.'

'That's understandable and I had no expectations…'

'But what I did know was that I didn't want you to change your plans for me.'

'I didn't really *have* plans as such.'

He went on as if she hadn't spoken. 'As you know, I am bound to this place and as much as I love it here, have come to love what I do, I spent a lot of time resenting it, resenting the circumstances that brought me back here before I was ready. I didn't want that for you. Didn't want to risk that if things didn't work out, you would feel the same way, regret you didn't get the chance to try new things and new places. Tie you down when you had just got free. But I should have given you that choice.'

Where was this going? 'Thank you, I appreciate that.'

'At the same time I was thrown. You had been so clear about what you wanted from me, about what we were, were the one to lay down the terms of our relationship that when you said…' He paused for a long time until she felt compelled to fill the silence.

'When I said I loved you.'

He nodded. ‘When you said that I didn’t know what to think. How *I* felt. I told myself I needed more time, I needed to figure out who I was without the commitments I had carried for so long before I was ready for any new commitment.’

‘Luciano, I know all this. Why go over it all again? I understood, I understand, and I have never demanded anything from you that you weren’t ready to give.’ Until now, maybe. ‘What are you trying to say?’

Luciano stared fixedly into the distance, a muscle ticking in his taut jaw. ‘I missed you. From the moment you left. I missed you.’

Hope sprang up, delicate and new. ‘I missed you too.’

‘I missed your smile and your questions and your laugh. I missed your voice, the very scent of you, the way you felt under my fingertips. I missed the way you sit on desks rather than on chairs and the way you look at me. I think…’ He swallowed, his jawline even tauter than ever. ‘I think I love you, I just didn’t recognise it. I didn’t know that it could creep up on a man like this. Not a thunderbolt but a slow realisation that you are everything that makes life meaningful. And I was too blind to realise what those feelings were. To realise that love isn't a trap but a gift and it doesn't mean life stays static. I should have told you that I love you back. Told you that there is always a place for you here no matter where you travelled to. But I was afraid. I lost everything eight years ago and it took me a long time to rebuild my life. I didn't want to disturb the fragile equilibrium. To risk losing someone else. But not acting is a loss too.' He grimaced. 'I am making a real mess of this.'

Liv sank onto the bench trying to process what she had just heard, to try to untangle his torrent of words. 'You love me?'

'Back then, in Florence, I used to look out for you, linger in the hope of running into you. My day was always a little brighter when you were in it. I valued our friendship, but I knew I wanted more. When I woke up that morning, before I saw the messages, I was elated, but also scared. Because I knew that what we shared could be life changing and I didn't know if I was ready for that. It was the same in the autumn. I knew if I named my feelings, allowed myself to admit how I felt, then nothing would be the same again and I wasn't ready to face that. But I should have faced it and I'm sorry.' He looked fully at her then, finally. 'And I am fully prepared for this to be the moment where you tell me that you fell in love with a backpacker and eloped and I am far too late.'

She laughed then. 'No, no backpacker. But I do have something to tell you, the reason I am here and not in Asia.' It was her turn to pause, to search for the words but in the end there was only one thing she could say. 'I'm pregnant, Luciano. I am having a baby. We are having a baby.'

She couldn't look at him. If admitting he loved her was a struggle, then how would he react to something so life changing?

'A baby?' he repeated blankly. 'But how? When?'

'How, well the usual way. I know we were careful but clearly not careful enough. When? I am not sure exactly but I am just over twelve weeks so late October sometime.' Those feverish nights of saying goodbye. 'I realised about ten days ago when Max called me to tell Annabel was pregnant. I flew home the next day to see the doctor and take some time to think about what happens next. Telling you was my first priority, I just didn't know how. But Luciano, the first thing you need to know is that I want this baby. I know it's mad and we live in two different countries and I am out of work, but I do. I knew that straight away, what that means for you is up to you. Look.' She got to her feet. 'This is a shock, I know. I don't expect you to react now. Or at all. I haven't come here with an agenda, wanting a certain outcome, but of course you need to know. Have a right to know.' She looked at him, pale and unmoving. 'I am going to go back to the Castello to give you some time. If you'd rather I go straight back to London and give you longer to absorb this then just say.'

He didn't reply, just nodded and Liv paused, desperately wanting to touch him, but instead she just made herself smile and say, 'Come find me when you are ready. Take as long as you need.' Then she turned and made her way back down the path towards the Castello. It was done. What happened next was down to Luciano.

But the hope was still there, still fragile, still new. He loved her. He regretted not telling her that before. He had reached out to her and all this before she had told him about the baby. For now that was enough.

Luciano heard Liv tell him she was heading back, that she was giving him space, but he couldn't react, couldn't move, his brain and body too busy processing the news.

Liv was pregnant. He was going to be a father. Not some day in the future but very soon. He sank onto the bench and stared unseeingly out at the view. *'Un bambino, Papa.'* He didn't realise he had spoken aloud until a small bird perched in the cherry tree flew off in alarm at the noise. Luciano reached out and touched the bark. 'You are going to be a grandfather.'

What did this mean? For Liv, for him, for them? He had only just come to terms with how he felt about her in the here and now; the future had seemed too vast to contemplate. He had thought he might spend some time with her on her travels, embrace the digital-nomad lifestyle every now and then, work from overseas when possible, hope that she might choose to return to Tuscany, to him when she had visited all the places she had wanted to see. And that had been the best-case scenario. The worst case she had already moved on, his declaration too little too late.

He inhaled. Nearly four months ago he had sat on this very bench and told Liv he wasn't ready for any commitment. That he had spent the last eight years shouldering responsibilities he had not been in any way ready for, raising a sister who had needed him in every way, allowing him no time to figure out anything apart from surviving the day-to-day. Freedom had felt like a reward. A reward for those early days of figuring out the business, fighting for the respect of the workers, of other winemakers and merchants, understanding the vast holdings the family had accumulated whilst managing Elisabetta's rehabilitation, physical and mental, and dealing with his own often repressed grief, his own emotions a luxury he couldn't manage.

But that was then and freedom wasn't the same for thirty-two-year-old Luciano as it had been for the twenty-four-year-old. He had matured during those years, been shaped by them. What was he realistically going to do apart from continue to make wine, manage the estate, worry about his sister no matter where she was and how old she was because that was what love meant? He didn't want to date, to be part of the rich Tuscany set with their parties and hedonism. He didn't want any woman but Liv. Even painting was now a hobby, not a vocation, as maybe it always should have been, as he had always would have realised one day, as his father had hoped, as Meg had known.

'How can I do this without you to guide

me?' he asked his father and Meg, as he so often did when he came here but he knew the answer. Just as he had done everything else he had had to do without their wisdom and advice. One day at a time, drawing on the sixteen years he had spent with them, the example they had set. It hadn't been enough time but it was all he had. What would they say if they were here? They would be telling him to stop sitting around thinking and to go and find Liv, to tell her it was going to be okay, to shoulder his responsibilities like the man they had raised him to be. The man he had grown into. The father he was going to be.

A baby. Maybe with Liv's grey eyes and his dark curls, or her strawberry blonde hair and his brown eyes. His and Liv's child. All at once all the shock faded away, replaced by a joy so fierce and euphoric it filled every fibre, every sinew. He and Liv were going to have a baby together and it felt right, deep in his bones it felt right, that this was where he had been heading all along; he had just been too blind to see it.

He reached out and touched both trees, solemnly, reverently, his ancestral Roman blood honouring those who had gone before, and then, without a backwards look, made his way back to the Castello.

It didn't take him long to find Liv. She was in her old room, curled up on the chaise, a book closed in her hand. She was pale under the tan and he was aware of the deep shadows under her eyes, the worry in her expression as she heard him come in. He should have reacted quicker, better, reassured her at once.

'I'm sorry,' he said aware that all he seemed to have done since she returned was apologise.

'For what?'

'For not telling you straight away how wonderful this news is, how wonderful you are.'

He saw the worry fade away, although the hope that replaced it was tinged with a wariness he knew he deserved. 'Don't apologise. I don't want platitudes or for you to tell me what you think I want or need to hear, for you to force anything. This was a huge shock for me, it must be the same for you.'

'It was at first, for a few minutes, but then as it sank in I realised that actually I was hoping I would hear those words one day. That if things turned out the way I hoped they would then this was where we were heading. It's all just happening a little quicker than expected'

'Do you mean that?'

'Absolutely. First I had intended to tell you that I loved you, and thank goodness I did before you told me you were pregnant.' Otherwise, she might have thought it a reaction to her news, not genuine. A lesson in not holding back that had nearly come too late. He knelt beside the chaise and took her hands in his. 'First, I told you that I loved you, then we spent a year or so seeing where that took us while you figured out what you wanted to do, where you wanted to be, and hopefully the answer would have been right here, because goodness knows, no one else could manage Betta's filing system. And then some time later I would have asked you to marry me and you would have said yes…'

She laughed at that. 'You seem very sure of yourself.'

'I wouldn't ask until I *was* sure. Then we would have got married and sometime after that you would tell me we were having a baby. You just fast-forwarded through most of that.'

'I didn't do it alone,' she said.

'*We* fast-forwarded. And why not? What does the order matter? What matters is that I love you, that I am in awe of you and what you are creating.'

'The baby is the size of a plum.'

'A plum?'

'According to Max, he and Annabel are using some kind of fruit measuring system.'

'A plum,' he repeated reverently. He looked at her stomach; it still looked flat to him, maybe the slightest curve. 'May I?'

'There's nothing to feel yet, the baby won't move for a while yet, but of course.' She took his hand and laid it on her stomach. 'Hello, *piccolino*,' he said softly.

'Or *piccolina*.'

'Or *piccolina*,' he agreed. He left his hand there for a little longer, feeling the rise and fall of her stomach as she breathed, aware of her gaze on him. Aware that he needed to get this right, to leave her in no doubt of his reaction.

'Liv,' he said as he straightened, still kneeling, taking her hands again. 'Whatever you decide, wherever you want to be I will support you. I hope you know that, believe that. It's been a long day. Why don't you get some rest, and we can talk more, properly over dinner?'

'That would be good, thank you. I am pretty tired.'

'*Bene*. I'll see you soon.' He stood up, then dropped a kiss onto her cheek. 'Let me know if you need anything at all.'

'I will, thank you.'

Luciano walked to the door then paused and turned back to her. 'It's all going to be fine, Liv. I promise you that.'

Liv felt a lot brighter after her nap and joined Luciano in the kitchen to help prepare dinner. They hadn't spent time like this before, the separation of what they did in private and the rest of their lives too acute, and despite her uncertainty about where the evening and conversation would go, she was impressed by his culinary skills. She diced tomatoes under his patient tutelage despite protesting that she knew how to make a pasta sauce, and ran through all the foods she was supposed to avoid and those she had taken an aversion too. Upon hearing she was still nauseated by the smell of wine 'not ideal in a vineyard, I know' Luciano replaced the bottle of red he had selected for himself back in the wine rack and poured some water instead despite her insisting it was fine. They avoided discussing the future while they cooked, instead she told him about the places she had visited during her briefer than expected travels, and he in turn discussed Elisabetta's decision to stay in New Zealand for the foreseeable future and attend university there.

'How do you feel about that?' she asked him.

'I miss her. But I'm glad she's moving on, getting to know her mother's country.'

'So that means you have a vacancy for an events manager?'

'Know anyone interested?'

'I might so. Would it be a deal breaker if the applicant was pregnant?'

He just smiled, ladling the pasta and the fragrant sauce into pasta bowls, setting a bowl of salad and a loaf of crusty bread in the middle of the table. Liv took a seat.

'This smells good. Thank you.'

They continued to chat about her family, Elisabetta's plans, and everything that had happened at the Castello over the last few months while they ate and it wasn't until Liv had regretfully turned down a second helping that Luciano broached the subject which had hung over them all evening.

'Liv, I have obviously been doing a lot of thinking. I know you have your own ideas of what the next few months, longer, may look like and I will of course support you in that. If that means getting a place in London and coming over every month, every fortnight, whatever then that is what I will do. But I would like you to stay. Not just because of the baby, but because it feels to me that you belong here, that you make this place a home.

Her heart stuttered at the warmth in his voice, in his eyes.

'You can take up your old job until the baby comes, and after if you wish, or not. You could live here as you did before, with your own rooms, and we can co parent but I would like it very much if you were here as my *fidanzata*. For now at least. One day I would very much like it if you were here as my wife. And Liv, I need you to believe this. If there were no baby I would be asking you this just the same. I love you and I want to make a life with you.'

'I believe you.' She did, she had no more lingering doubts. 'And I love you too. You are right, this place does feel like my home. It did from the very first. I love being here, I love my work, I love what you do and the people you work with, the countryside. And I love you. Coming back here for good, to work and to live and to raise our baby together is the path I was searching for all this time, I just didn't realise it. I want to make a life with you and see where that leads us.'

'You're sure?'

'I really am,' she took his hand. 'I don't think we should rush into getting engaged, into getting married, things are already moving so fast, and this baby is commitment enough. Ask me, if you still want to, when we have had weeks of sleepless nights because the baby is teething, you have the harvest to bring in and I have the wedding party from hell.' It wasn't that she didn't want to marry him, she did, but there was so much change, so much that was new. She wanted to slow down, to savour each step as much as she could.

'It's a deal.' Luciano stood up, drawing her to her feet and into his arms. 'Welcome home, Liv.'

'I'm glad to be home.' And as he kissed her she knew there would be nowhere else she would rather be.

# EPILOGUE

IT HAD BEEN a warm, dry October. The harvest was in, the grapes crushed and starting on their journey towards becoming wine, the year's walking parties and business events and weddings done. Except for one.

Luciano was used to seeing his home decorated for celebrations, to seeing the pergola in the walled garden bedecked with seasonal flowers, the chairs lined up for guests dressed in their best, or whatever dress code had been dictated by brides and groom more interested in the aesthetic than their family and friends' comfort. He was used to seeing fairy lights strewn through the trees, the flooring laid for dancing, tables set for dining.

He just wasn't used to seeing it decorated for him. For him to be the one dressed in a new, formal suit, tie matching those of his father-in-law-to-be, brother-in-law-to-be and his own close friends. He wasn't used to being the one at the centre of the pre wedding dinners and festivities. To be the one reciting his vows and speech silently, determined to get it right, determined to give Liv the day she deserved.

'Here you are. See, Margherita, I told you Papa was nearby.' He turned to see Max, in matching suit and tie, holding a toddler in each arm. Cousins, born just a few weeks apart one summer ago. He reached out and took his daughter from her uncle, smoothing the skirts of her flower girl dress and adjusting the circlet of flowers on her head, kissing her cheek as he did so.

'Ciao, bella.' He reached out to touch the other girl's cheek. 'You look beautiful, Persephone.'

'Give them both ten minutes,' Max said with a grin. 'I told Liv she was crazy putting this pair of monkeys in white silk.'

'Which is why your mother has two pairs of jeans and tops ready to change them as soon as the ceremony and photos are over.' Lucino looked over at the chairs, now almost filled, where Liv's mother sat in the front row, a capacious bag at her feet holding everything that two adventurous toddlers might need.

'My mother is nothing but prepared.' Max

gave him a knowing look. 'Nervous? I thought I was going to throw up before I married Annabel.'

'Actually, no,' Luciano said slowly. 'Just ready for the rest of our lives to begin.' He kissed his daughter one more time than handed her over to his sister and went to take his place in the pergola and await his bride.

Funny to have coordinated so many weddings and only now realise why so many brides got hung up on a myriad details. But there was nothing to worry about. Everything was perfect from the weather through to the string quartet currently playing one of her favourite concertos. Liv took in a deep breath and took her bouquet from her sister. Portia was maid of honour, her daughter and niece flower girls and Elisabetta the one bridesmaid.

'Okay,' Elisabetta said, appearing with a small girl in each hand. 'They are both still clean and happy which is a miracle so let's go. Oh Liv. You look beautiful. Luciano is going to swoon.'

'That's the plan.' Liv bent down to kiss her daughter and niece and then her sister-in-law-to-be. 'You look beautiful too, Betta. That pink is gorgeous on you.' She knew Luciano missed his sister, hated her being so far away, but New Zealand clearly suited her, she was relaxed and tanned and healthy, loving her course and the outdoor lifestyle. 'Okay,' as the music changed to the bridal march. 'Let's go.'

Afterwards Liv could only remember parts of the ceremony. The look in Luciano's eyes as she walked towards him, the tremor in her voice as she recited her vows, the moment Margherita toddled up and held out her arms demanding 'Up!'. The moment Luciano whispered 'ti amo'. She turned as they were pronounced man and wife and looked at her family and friends beaming at them, their daughter in her arms.

It had taken them ten years to get here, but this was exactly where they were supposed to be.

* * * * *

*If you loved* Hired for One Tuscan Summer *by Jessica Gilmore, look out for Jessica's next story, coming soon! And why not try some of her other recent titles:*

It Started with a Vegas Wedding
Miss Right All Along
Fake Date on the Orient Express